THE WITCH DOCTOR IS IN

WASHINGTON MEDICAL: VAMPIRE WARD, BOOK 1

MINDY KLASKY

RES IPSA PRESS

ALSO BY MINDY KLASKY

You can always find a complete, up-to-date list of Mindy's books (including books in other genres) on her website.

The Washington Witches Series (Magical Washington)

Girl's Guide to Witchcraft

Sorcery and the Single Girl

Magic and the Modern Girl

The Washington Witches Series, Volumes 1-3 (a boxed set containing *Girl's Guide to Witchcraft, Sorcery and the Single Girl,* and *Magic and the Modern Girl*)

Capitol Magic (a cross-over with the Washington Vampires Series)

Single Witch's Survival Guide

Joy of Witchcraft

"Dreaming of a Witch Christmas" (a Yule short story)

Nice Witches Don't Swear (a crossover with the Magic and Mayhem Kindle World, available only on Amazon in the US)

The Washington Vampires Series (Magical Washington)

Fright Court

Law and Murder

Capitol Magic (a cross-over with the Washington Witches Series)

"Stake Me Out to the Ball Game" (a short story published as part of the Uncollected Anthology)

Magic Times Two (*Fright Court* released in a two-for-one book duo with a novel by Deborah Blake)

~

The Washington Warders Series (Magical Washington)

The Library, the Witch, and the Warder

~

The Washington Medical Series (Magical Washington)

The Witch Doctor Is In

~

The As You Wish Series

"Wishful Thinking"

Act One, Wish One

Wishing in the Wings

Wish Upon a Star

The As You Wish Series (a boxed set containing *Act One, Wish One*, *Wishing in the Wings*, and *Wish Upon a Star*)

This is a work of fiction. Any references to historical events, real people, or real locales are used fictitiously. Other names, characters, places, and incidents are products of the author's imagination, and any resemblance to actual events or locales or persons, living or dead, is entirely coincidental.

Cover design by Renée George

Published by Res Ipsa Press
P.O. Box 1624, Cedar Crest, NM 87008-1624

Discover other titles by Mindy Klasky at www.mindyklasky.com

051818mkm

1

First do no harm—that's what they taught me in medical school.

Maybe being a witch kept me from mastering that lesson. Because there I was, standing in my office at Empire General Hospital, contemplating an awful lot of harm—both physical and magical—to my not-so-innocent familiar. I stared at an envelope addressed to Medical Director Ashley McDonnell, with a postmark indicating the letter had been sent three months earlier.

"Musker!" I roared, even though my lazy familiar was only a few feet away.

In lieu of a return address, an enchanted logo flickered in the envelope's upper left corner—an animated snake writhing around a wooden staff and flicking its tongue in warning. The letter came from the Eastern Empire Healthcare Facilities Accreditation Board.

"Musker!" I hollered again. My familiar was responsible for sorting my mail, making sure I saw my most pressing correspondence first. Alas, Musker was as well-suited to being an executive assistant as I was to winning the Indy 500.

But beggars—and medical directors of severely underfunded hospitals for supernatural creatures—couldn't be choosers.

I narrowed my eyes, barely resisting the urge to set fire to the correspondence. The contents inside were probably charmed against burning, spindling or mutilating, but the last thing I needed was to set off the overhead sprinklers.

Holding my breath, I ripped open the envelope with a letter opener shaped like a miniature athame. Applying the replica of a magical knife to paper was the closest I'd come to ritual witchcraft for weeks. Running Empire General, with its seemingly endless series of disasters, had seen to that.

My gaze flicked over the formal missive inside.

Upcoming one-year anniversary of Empire General... Substantial concerns about long-term financial viability... Additional concerns about the physical health of diverse imperial patients... Team of inspectors will arrive at midnight on Midsummer Eve.

Midnight.

Midsummer Eve.

One month from tonight.

"Musker!" I bellowed one more time, stomping across my office and shoving open the door to my en suite bathroom.

Yeah, the bathroom was supposed to be a perk of the job—one tiny advantage to lure qn unsuspecting doctor to take on the impossible task of running Empire General. The on-site housing (former servants' quarters in the converted mansion that housed the hospital) sure wasn't a draw. And the three meals a day (hospital food—pretty much as bad as you're thinking. No. Worse.) weren't anything to write home about.

But the bathroom—marble floor, walk-in shower, heated towel racks, and a programmable toilet, for Hecate's sake!—the *bathroom* was supposed to make me love my job. Except my good-for-nothing familiar had taken over the room our first day on the premises.

Shoving open the door, I was swatted in the face by a wall of desert air.

I blinked in the orange-red glow of the overhead heat lamps as sweat broke out along my hairline. Inlaid coils in the marble floor gave off shimmering waves like a desert mirage. Whoever had designed the high-end sweatbox had never meant it to be cranked to eleven in late May.

Whoever had designed the high-end sweatbox had never met my familiar.

"You rang?" Musker crooned, blinking slowly as he swiveled his head toward the door. He was ensconced in a padded chaise lounge, exposing nearly every inch of his muscled body to the merciless glow overhead. A tiny bronze-colored Speedo preserved his modesty. No. Wait. Musker *had* no modesty. He only wore the bathing suit to keep his most sensitive flesh from sticking to the chair.

"How can you—"

"Do you mind?" Musker interrupted. "You're letting all the hot air out."

I was his witch. He was subordinate to me in all matters magical and mundane. After eighteen years of bonded partnership, we both knew the rules, even if I'd been too busy for months to work even the simplest spell.

I stepped inside the sauna and closed the door behind me.

Musker stretched his neck in approval. I brandished the accreditation letter and shouted, "I just found this on my desk!"

His broad mouth curved in a smile. "I worked late last night, sorting the mail."

"This was sent three months ago!"

A lazy blink. "There was a lot to go through."

"We could have spent the past twelve weeks preparing for inspection! There's only one month left before the accreditation board gets here!"

Musker shifted on his chair, exposing more of his lean flank to the overhead heat. "You know as well as I do that things will just come undone if you start organizing *too* early."

"I know nothing of the sort!" My voice echoed off the marble walls. "We have records to file! Inventories to complete! Patient histories—"

"Blah, blah, blah," Musker said, his eyelids drooping as if he were about to fall asleep.

I should have summoned my powers to fry his lizard skin. I should have thrown him out the hospital's front door into the dark and rainy night. I should have let him sleep under a cold and clammy rock forever.

But I couldn't do any of that.

Lazy or not, Musker was my familiar. I'd chosen him my second year at the Washington Magicarium, selecting his reliquary from among all the containers stored at my school. Other girls had chosen traditional cats. Some had been swayed by sweet little familiars—bunnies or hedgehogs. A few had been attracted to powerful creatures like mastiffs or bears.

I'd chosen a lizard.

I'd chosen a lizard because the reliquary was dusty and shoved all the way to the back of the shelf. The container had clearly sat there for years, maybe even for generations. I felt sorry for the creature inside, even as I asked myself what young witch would choose to have a *lizard* as her constant companion?

The same girl who insisted on studying American history, along with her daily courseload of spells, runes, herbs, and crystals. The same girl—woman—who decided to go to medical school even after her mother begged her not to. (Begged and berated and downright forbade, because medical school just wasn't *done*. There were too many conflicts between witchy ways and modern science. Hecate didn't play well with the Hippocratic Oath.)

I'd been a rebel from the day I threw my first rattle out of my bassinet.

"Let's go," I said to Musker.

He swiveled his head in sluggish consideration. "Where?"

"My office. *Now.*"

My familiar might have been the laziest creature in the entire Eastern Empire. But he recognized a command from his witch when he heard one. With surprising speed, he skittered across the room toward the heated towel rack. His clothes were draped over the metal bars—a much-wrinkled khaki shirt that looked like it belonged on a safari guide and a matching pair of disreputable trousers. He slipped his feet into brown sandals, letting his toes curl over the ends like claws.

We both shivered as we returned to my office. I was grateful for the breathable air, but Musker hunched beside my desk, glaring balefully at the countless manila folders stacked there.

"First things first," I said brightly, determined to ignore his bad attitude. "Let's send a response to the Board, telling them we look forward to their visit."

I reached for a sheet of Empire General stationery. The hospital's logo was stamped across the top—a spray of stars twisted into a stethoscope. Hmmm... I could zap the design with a dose of magic and make the stars dance when the bureaucrats opened my reply.

Musker's tongue flicked out in a gesture of distaste, but he shifted closer to my side. I settled my palm over his ropy forearm as I closed my eyes. Before I could summon the words of an animating spell, though, I shifted my position. My neck was still sweating from the bathroom heat. I twisted my hair into a messy bun, stabbing it into place with a convenient ball-point pen.

Taking a deep breath, I settled back in my oversize leather chair. This time, I brushed my fingertips against Musker's ready palm. I'd energized dozens of designs in the past—my graduation announcement from the Washington Magicarium, invitations to potluck parties, a baby shower for a witchy friend.

I was tired, though. Hungry, too. I'd missed dinner—such as it was, with glue-like chipped beef on toast billed as the nightly special. (No, the printed menus didn't announce the sticky consistency. Eleven months of hard-won experience warned me away.) Instead, I'd spent the time walking the hospital hallways and checking on patients. Twenty-four of our thirty beds were occupied, and we were treating our first sprite ever—

Concentrate.

Another deep breath as I turned back to the letterhead. I touched my free fingers to my forehead, offering up the power of my thoughts to Hecate. I touched my throat, offering up the power of my voice. I touched my chest, just above the xiphoid process, offering up the power of my heart.

"Goddess help me spark this drawing,

Aid me with this mundane task.

So I might greet all with magic,

So I might serve where you ask."

Nothing happened. There wasn't the familiar *flash* of darkness, the moment when the mundane world was blocked by sheer arcane power. The design on the letterhead didn't shift. Not a single star moved.

Disconcerted, I scooted to the front of my chair. That new position allowed me to settle the whole length of my arm against Musker's. I repeated my breathing and centering. I closed my eyes to increase my concentration, and I recited my spell again.

Nothing. Not even a tickle of magic, the feather-soft thread of energy that had made me sneeze every single time I worked the Rota during my first three years in school.

Suddenly anxious, I stood, taking care to plant my feet squarely on the floor. I tried to swallow in my suddenly bone-dry throat. I clamped my fingers on Musker's shoulder.

My initial grip was hard enough to make him wince. It took a conscious effort to ease back.

Three deep breaths. Thoughts, voice, heart. Familiar doggerel spell...

I stopped after three words. Magic should have welled up as I began my chant—*Goddess help me*. I should have felt Hecate's holy gift vibrate through every cell in my body.

But even more than that, I should have felt my familiar beside me. His energy should have thrummed against mine, catching even the faintest hint of my power and mirroring it back like sunlight amplified across acres of desert sand.

Musker had centered me for every substantial working I'd tried since his awakening. He'd steadied me. He'd buoyed me to accomplish more than I'd ever imagined was possible.

He was my familiar, sworn and true. And right now, in the middle of the night, in the heart of the building I was sworn to administer and protect, I couldn't feel even a hint of his presence.

I couldn't sense my familiar.

I couldn't reach my magic.

I was ruined as a witch.

2

Use it or lose it.

That was the rule with magic. Spend too much time away from established workings, and Hecate's gift leached away.

I knew that. I'd learned it in the magicarium. I'd just never thought the restriction would apply to *me*.

A clinical part of my mind monitored my reaction to my failure. My heart rate rose. I started to hyperventilate, breathing too rapidly to allow my alveoli to perfuse oxygen into my bloodstream. My fingertips grew numb, likely a result of my hyperventilation.

My witchy soul screamed questions. How long had it been since I'd worked a spell? Organizing papers in my office. Reheating a cup of tea. Making my bed in my tiny bedroom upstairs?

But years of interacting with humans at medical school had retrained my witchy brain. I'd long since abandoned the everyday spells my arcane sisters took for granted, because I dared not risk exposure.

Still, I must have undertaken some major ritual recently. The magical year was filled with them.

Alas, I'd skipped celebrating Beltane with the Washington Coven just a few weeks before. Spring at the hospital was insanely busy, with hypersexualized dryads responding to rising sap by seeking mates (and occasionally breaking limbs), with bellicose centaurs fighting for territory as they started to rut (and occasionally breaking limbs), and with gnomes excavating substantially deeper tunnels once the danger of frost was past (and occasionally breaking limbs).

Of course, spring wasn't just about setting bones. There were the usual challenges of vampires caught by the longer days and griffins brought low by the near-constant rainfall, and gargoyles worn out by the constant shifts in temperature.

Even earlier in the year, Ostara had been a hopeless cause for magic rituals because the sabbat had coincided with a full moon. A host of shifters had kept the ER busy for a full forty-eight hours, including an entire litter of first-time wolves who couldn't manage their transition back to human form without a little pharmaceutical assistance.

Imbolc...

Yule...

Had I really not worked a spell since *Samhain*? I could remember arriving late for the Washington Coven's rite on Halloween, and I'd left before socializing began. Surely, I'd spoken the ritual words with my sisters by sheer force of habit, even if I couldn't remember invoking the Guardians or lighting candles. I must have asked Hecate's blessing for the arcane new year. Hadn't I?

As if he'd followed my grim calculation, a shiver ran down Musker's body, starting at the crest of his sleek bald head and ending at the base of his spine. His tongue darted out over his lips. He leaned into me, pressing his whole body against my side, but I couldn't say if he was seeking comfort or giving it. Or maybe he'd simply grown cold outside the hothouse of his adapted bathroom.

Before either of us could say anything, a tone shrilled from the speaker set against the crown molding in my office—three brief blasts, followed by a deadpan message: "Code Grey in the ER. Code Grey, ER. Stat."

Code Yellow meant a patient was missing.

Code Blue meant an adult was in cardiac arrest.

Code Grey meant a security threat, a combative person with no obvious weapon on his or her person. Of course, in a hospital for supernatural creatures, *obvious* weapons were the least dangerous kind.

I ran for the Emergency Room.

Actually, I ran to the ER entrance—just across the lobby from my office. Before I could burst into the treatment area, I was stopped by my warder, Rebecca Sartain. "Let Security do their job," Becs said.

Security was a hormone-addled centaur yearling and a senescent gargoyle. "We're understaffed tonight," I snapped. "Dr. Hart might need my help!"

"She might," Becs agreed. "You'll know for sure as soon as Mikaela and Jerome have things under control."

"I'm the medical director of this hospital!" I raised my voice over a sudden crash in the ER.

"Of course you are," my warder said, shifting her weight when I tried to push past her. She had six inches on me and fifty pounds, all of it muscle. If anyone else had tried to shove their way into the ER, Becs would have summoned her sword from the ether. But no warder ever pulled a weapon on her witch.

Rebecca Sartain followed rules a lot better than I did. Maybe that's why we were best friends—opposites attract. Or maybe it was because I'd known she was a girl in boy's clothing the first time I saw her at one of the awkward school dances held between her warders' academy and my witches' magicarium. Her buzz-cut hair and clenched fists hadn't fooled me for a second. By the time we both graduated, there hadn't been a shadow of a hint of an inkling of doubt about who I'd choose to protect me. I'd never considered anyone but Becs.

Now, I clicked my tongue like an exasperated teenager and craned my neck for a view into the ER. Another loud crash sounded from somewhere inside.

"Becs!" I would have reached for my power to emphasize my command, but I didn't have that option. I resorted to pleading, "Please!"

Becs swore and gestured for Musker to fall in behind me. Summoning her sword, she led the way into the ER.

In the center of the room, a man snarled like a mad dog—a six-foot-tall dog with linebacker shoulders, an impressive five o'clock shadow, and a swirl of tattoos across his massive forearms. A pair of worn jeans sat low on his hips, his belt buckle glinting like the bow on a present for a very good girl. His tight black T-shirt spelled out every ridge of his abs.

The sudden giddy-up of my heart had nothing to do with the fact that Empire General's newest patient was methodically trying to take out my security guards, turning a cluster of EKG leads into a whirling set of nunchucks.

Mikaela, the young centaur, tried to dart forward. She was intent on corralling the patient in Bay Three until he flicked the leads at her head, shouting a wordless syllable. Mikaela reared back. Bad luck landed her foot on the electrical cord of the abused EKG machine. Her teeth clacked shut as she sat down hard.

Jerome peered at his fellow guard through rheumy eyes. The gargoyle looked like he'd just awakened from deep sleep—which he probably had. He never made it through an entire night shift without a nap. Or two. Or three.

Now, he cleared his throat, making a sound like a fall of scree down a bare mountainside. He addressed his words to the rampaging patient. "You don't want to hurt anyone, son. Just put those leads down. We've got doctors here who can help you."

"Where the hell am I?" the man growled.

Jerome blinked, and for just a moment I worried he'd forgotten the answer. He should have retired years earlier, but financial planning was tricky for creatures who lived five hundred years. He needed the salary, and Empire General was supposed to be an easy job.

"You're in the hospital, son," Jerome finally rattled. "Best place for you right now in the entire Eastern Empire. We help people like you every day, um, night."

Mikaela climbed to her feet, clumsy with the pain of her pratfall. Nevertheless, she started to circle around to the patient's far side, probably planning to draw his attention so Jerome could jump him from behind.

The strategy was iffy from the beginning, doubly so because my geriatric gargoyle guard wasn't jumping anywhere. The patient flicked his leads again, driving Mikaela back three whole steps.

The motion gave me my first glimpse of the man's right side. More exactly, of the right side of his throat. And to be most precise, the torn and bleeding tissue around his mangled right jugular.

Realization dawned. Sure enough, I caught a whiff of cinnamon, likely from the dark stain across the front of his T-shirt. A rusty smear ran from the man's mouth to his chin.

No. Not man.

Vampire.

The torn neck told me he'd been attacked by a vampire. The flaking residue around his mouth said he'd bitten back. He'd consumed vampire blood—enough to turn him from his human state. And the cinnamon-scented stain across his chest announced that someone had dosed him with Lethe, the elixir all vampires carried to force mere humans to forget they'd come in contact with the supernatural.

That gave the guy a chance to remain mortal.

Lethe slowed human metabolism. If he'd been dosed with enough... If he'd only swallowed a little blood... If the Lethe had kept the vampire contagion from reaching his heart...

There might still be time to dose him with Vitriol.

A thousand times more costly than plutonium, Vitriol was a brutal potion, made possible only by the rare cooperation of elementals. Gnomes mined the raw materials near veins of sulfur beneath extinct volcanos. Ifrit worked some obscure form of fire magic, converting pungent yellow chalk to a blazing potion. Sylphs stirred the brew with their strongest breath, cooling the philter until it barely flowed. Undines summoned water from the deepest lakes in the world, adding drop by precious drop until the potion was perfectly balanced.

Vitriol could stop a human from turning into a vampire.

The only catch—aside from an eye-watering price—was that Vitriol caused infinitely more pain than the slash of a feeding vampire. The potion ravaged its way through every major organ system, corrupting every cell in the body. Some patients who survived the physical effects suffered permanent emotional trauma, leaving them worse off than if they'd never been dosed.

Even I, rule-breaker extraordinaire, would never administer Vitriol to a weakened patient or a child. But the Adonis who was even now destroying my ER by shoving Jerome into a fully loaded crash cart? He was strong enough to survive the potion, if anyone was.

I lunged for the drug safe by the nurse's station.

I'd rehearsed this drill. Every Empire General doctor had. With Becs and Musker at my back, I slammed my palm against the biometric lock. "Come on," I muttered, as if the words would make the sensing mechanism work more quickly. When the electronics finally flashed green, I placed my eye against the retinal scan and counted in my head: One Mississippi Two Mississippi Three Mississippi Four.

The lock silently released. I tugged with desperate hands,

forcing the lead-lined door to swing open. Following well-rehearsed protocol, I reached for the green vial, the one that was marked with a skull and crossbones and glowed with golden light from the life-saving elixir within.

But there was no golden light.

No skull. No crossbones. No green vial.

The safe was empty. Someone had stolen the only flask of Vitriol in all of Washington DC.

3

Gone.

The Vitriol was gone.

That was impossible. I'd checked it three and a half weeks before, working the biometric lock the way I did on the first of every month. Following procedure, I'd been accompanied by two other doctors. They'd countersigned my log, assuring the entire Eastern Empire that we had the remedy available.

Security cameras were focused on the drug safe day and night. Our small stock of Vitriol was worth half a year of Empire General's operating budget. That was the power vampires had over human imagination—we were willing to pay millions to save even one mundane from unwanted transition.

That, plus we knew the extraordinary street value for the drug. When Vitriol was injected by an imperial whose veins did *not* course with vampire blood, it gave an exquisite high, superior to any other drug, magic or mundane.

Now we'd never know if the man rampaging through my ER was strong enough to emerge from Vitriol unscathed.

I whirled around to find that my emergency room specialist, Dr. Hart, was finally taking charge. The sylph's face was weathered, as if she'd spent decades on the Russian steppes. Her hair and eyes were faded to a color without a name. Her doctor's coat was the unbroken blue of a wind-swept sky.

As Mikaela's and Jerome's attempts to secure the patient were cast off yet again, Dr. Hart raised cupped hands to her lips. Serenely, she exhaled hard into the space between her palms. Her fingers curled around her breath, snagging and shaping it.

Even as the man crouched in a renewed defensive stance, Dr. Hart flung her breath across the room. It gathered speed as it flew, spinning in upon itself. It struck the patient's wrist with all the concentrated force of a cyclone.

I winced, knowing that a human's bones would be shattered by the blow. The man, though, wouldn't be hampered by human bones. He'd have the benefit of a vampire's rapid healing in far too short a time.

His fingers spasmed as he tried to maintain his grip on the EKG leads, but they clattered to the floor. Mikaela pawed them to the side, taking care to avoid snagging them on the wheels of the crash cart.

"Enough," Dr. Hart said. Her voice blew across the room with determined certainty.

In response, my own heart rate slowed. The man relaxed into a fighter's crouch, still alert, still ready to defend himself, but no longer intent on laying waste to everyone in the room. He held his right arm at a stiff angle, clearly protecting his wrist.

Mikaela and Jerome backed off to the perimeter of the ER as Dr. Hart glided toward the intake desk. There, she picked up a leather wallet from amid a jumble of keys and a shoulder holster, complete with a pistol.

Flipping open the wallet, Dr. Hart revealed a golden badge—a five-pointed star with circles on the tip of each arm, surrounding a blue-and-red shield. An ID card glinted beneath a plastic flap.

"Nicholas Raines," Dr. Hart read.

The man's good hand curled into a fist, the strain of his tendons a sure sign that vampire blood was working its way through his veins. Or maybe he was merely contemplating his next break for freedom. Instead of trying to batter down the walls of my emergency room, he jutted his chin toward the desk and demanded, "How did you get my weapon?"

Dr. Hart breathed calm into her response, gesturing toward the cinnamon-scented stain on his shirt. "You gave it to us." Before he could shout his obvious outrage, she continued, "Certain compulsions were placed upon you before you were conveyed here."

"Where the hell is here?"

"You're in a hospital. You were attacked, but we're here to help."

The man raised one hand to his throat, but his fingertips came away dry. Vampire blood was already healing his body. His skin had knit to a fine sheen over his torn jugular. As he stared at his unmarked hand, Raines's voice ratcheted down. "What's happening to me?"

"You're turning into a vampire." Dr. Hart's words left no room for doubt, no space for disbelief. "There is no cure for your condition, but we *can* sedate you, which will allow you to avoid most of the pain of transition."

"I'm not afraid of pain." The words were a simple truth—not a boast or a taunt.

"As you wish," Dr. Hart said. "I'm afraid you can't be allowed contact with any human family or acquaintances now that transition is under way."

I knew Dr. Hart was simply delivering the law of the Empire—no human could ever learn of our supernatural existence.

I also knew there were exceptions to that law. More than one witch had confided her status to friends through the years. Warders too—a few had shared tales about the Academy, about the magic of the astral plane.

But vampires were especially cautious about revealing their existence to humans. Too many stakes had been pounded into undead hearts. Too many silver bullets had been fired over the centuries. Vampires were creatures of the night, born in fear and wrapped in terror.

"I understand," Raines said, which was more than most men could have managed under the circumstances.

"Very well. We have a private room for you upstairs where you can complete your transition. With your permission, we'll monitor your vital signs and collect data that will help us treat others."

She made this sound so normal, as if she were only obtaining informed consent for minor cosmetic surgery.

Our Vitriol was stolen! I wanted to shout. *Someone broke into Empire General and took our most valuable possession out of a locked safe!*

But Raines was talking again, asking exactly what would happen to him. Dr. Hart explained that his heart would stop. His lungs too. His muscles would transform, giving him ten times the strength and four times the speed he'd ever known as a human.

"And then I can find whoever did this to me?" His voice was very, very quiet.

"You're an imperial now, Mr. Raines. We have courts. Procedures. Processes. We do not tolerate revenge killings."

"No one said anything about killing." His voice was even lower. For just a heartbeat, I pitied the poor vampire who'd attacked him.

Dr. Hart, though, seemed unaffected by Raines's quiet rage. She floated a hand toward me. "Dr. McDonnell is in charge of Empire General. Just last month, she launched a new program designed to ease the transition you're currently experiencing."

That was my cue. Even as Becs rustled behind me with concern, I took a step closer to the Empire's newest vampire.

Forcing clinical distance into my voice, I said, "Let's get you settled upstairs before the sun rises."

I wasn't prepared for the furious glare Raines cast my way. His pupils were dilated, even in the bright light of the ER. His body was still awash in adrenaline, the *fight* he'd chosen over *flight*.

My "Welcome the Night" program—glossy brochures, professional videos, and a plushie shaped like a smiling fang—had seemed like a much better idea before I was confronted with my first unwilling vampire patient.

I cleared my throat and tried again. "Y— You can get some sleep. And our best counselors will be available to answer all your questions tomorrow night. We'll be with you every step of the way, until you take your first meal—"

Dr. Hart interrupted Raines's guttural snarl. "Come with me, Mr. Raines. Let's get you upstairs, and I'll see to your wrist. Your vampire blood will heal the break, but I want to make sure the bones are set properly."

That was clever, reminding him of her magic. She was a lot more convincing than my fledgling patient education campaign. Raines let himself be led to the vampire ward.

I recovered enough to snatch the black wallet from Dr. Hart's hand as she walked by. *Nicholas Raines*, the ID card said. *United States Secret Service*.

Holy crap!

No civilized vampire would feed from an unwilling source. And even a rogue who liked his meal on the hoof wasn't likely to go after someone as strong as Raines. How could a vampire have targeted a sworn officer of the most elite police force in the country? And why would the attacker bring a Lethe-dosed victim to our doorstep?

Vampires managed their own affairs. They controlled their scions, even the unwilling ones. *Especially* the unwilling ones.

I'd only launched my Welcome the Night program to attract an easy case or two. There were *some* planned transitions for willing scions. A few, anyway. Okay. I'd hoped we'd get one, at some point, somewhere down the line.

There was nothing like trial by fire, with a Secret Service agent as my first test case. I winced. Maybe *trial by fire* wasn't the best choice of words.

Shaking my head, I turned back to the empty drug safe. Welcome the Night wouldn't be on the line if our Vitriol hadn't been stolen. Before I could study the scene of the crime, Becs slipped up to my side. "Come on," she said. "Let's get you upstairs too."

"I have to report the theft!"

"Better to deal with the EBI in the morning."

My automatic protest was shattered by a jaw-breaking yawn. Ordinarily, I'd banish my fatigue with a spell. I knew the words well enough; I'd used them frequently—if surreptitiously—throughout medical school. But without my powers, I had no quick fix for exhaustion readily at hand.

And tiredness was the least of my problems. Without magic, I'd be hard-pressed to prepare for the accreditation board's inspection in four short weeks, condensing three months of work into one. And even *if* I figured out a way to kickstart my magic, the hospital inspection was placed in grave danger by the Vitriol theft.

If the hospital failed inspection I'd be fired. Job hunting would be infinitely complicated by my inability to explain where I'd been working for the previous year. Potential employers would assume I was a problem case—drugs or emotional instability or embezzlement of funds. I had to be hiding *something*.

Something besides the existence of a secret paranormal world thriving in the middle of Washington DC.

"Let's go," Becs insisted. "And you—" She nodded toward Musker, who stood by the door with a wary expression on his face. "Get some sleep, too."

My slothful familiar didn't need to be told twice. He sidled toward my office and his heated marble palace.

I let my best friend guide me into the lobby. I didn't argue as we crossed to the tiny elevator retrofitted into the mansion walls. I watched as she pushed the button for 4, and I let her walk me down the narrow corridor to my tiny attic room. She hung my white doctor's coat on the hook behind my door, and I handed her my shoes to tuck inside the narrow armoire that served as my closet.

She'd helped me countless times before, when I'd pushed my powers past the point of no return. There was an easy familiarity as she turned back my comforter and plumped my pillow.

But I hadn't used my powers to excess that night. I might never use my powers again. Starting to panic, I said, "I— I have to—"

"Everything will look better after you get some rest." Becs touched the center of my forehead. I protested, but she said, "*Sleep.*" She reinforced the suggestion with a healthy measure of warder's magic.

At least one of us till had her powers.

Unable to resist her compulsion, I slept.

4

My warder was a wise and wonderful woman. As Becs predicted, everything *was* better when I woke. Of course, that might have had something to do with the fact that I slept for ten straight hours.

It was a good thing I'd served my residency in the emergency room. My body no longer cared if I went to bed at six in the morning and woke at four in the afternoon. Sleep was sleep—rejuvenating no matter what the clock said.

Getting dressed, alas, was another matter entirely.

For the past eleven months, I'd barely thought about clothes. Each morning, I pulled on a clean set of scrubs and my white doctor's coat. The hospital laundry kept me fighting fit.

But for some reason, I wasn't satisfied with scrubs that afternoon. Okay, I knew perfectly well that the reason was about six feet tall with two hundred pounds of pure muscle, made even more delectable by lips that were permanently set just a few degrees shy of a frown...

That was ridiculous. Nicholas Raines was my *patient*. He'd just been put through the wringer, forcibly undertaking a transition that was literally nightmare material for nearly every human alive.

And I wasn't some naive woman who'd never seen a man before. I'd lost my virginity at magicarium prom my senior year, handing over the honors to Caden Park, a gawky warder with a lot more speed than skill. I'd dated a couple of guys at Harvard, at least until they started asking too many questions. *No* doctor had time to date during med school—that didn't make me a freak.

I'd experienced the flutter of hormones well before Nicholas Raines showed up in my emergency room. Still, no law said a woman had to dress like a sack of potatoes.

My black silk sheath was a little much, even if I *was* working the night shift. My winter white jersey knit would last about seven seconds before it attracted a stain. My pencil skirt was cute and would give me that certain sexy-librarian-je-ne-sais-quoi, but even I wasn't crazy enough to think I could wear its accompanying sexy heels for a full eight-hour shift.

That was it. The total contents of my wardrobe, aside from yoga pants, T-shirts, and some ancient rejects wrinkled in the back corner. Sweet Hecate, I needed to get out more.

I pulled on a baggy pair of green cotton scrubs and tied a floppy bow at my waist. Maybe makeup would make the difference I craved. I found my mascara at the back of the drawer beside my sink. Smoky eyeliner, too. There. That was an improvement—as long as I didn't have a sudden crying jag.

Encouraged by my makeup success, I tested out a small spell—just a little something to bring out the buttery highlights in my hair. I completed my deep breaths with all the attention of a first-year magicarium student. I centered my fingertips on my forehead, at the base of my larynx, and directly above my heart.

I didn't bother with the spell, though. I could feel the complete lack of magic, the utter absence of power in my arcane reservoir. Before I could despair, I headed down to the kitchen for breakfast. Dinner. Whatever I was supposed to call the late afternoon meal that was my first food after waking.

Rather than summon Natasha, the rusalka who ran the kitchen, I decided to fend for myself, throwing together a couple of slices of toast and a bowl of strawberries. It couldn't be worse than the fare our professional cook would create.

Well, that was a lie. One piece of toast was burned, and the other was still soft bread. I was probably a worse cook than Natasha—a truly terrifying prospect. At least the berries were perfect.

I'd run out of excuses. It was time to visit my patient. I headed upstairs to the hospital's second floor and the vampire ward.

Steel double doors closed behind me, locking out any hint of daylight that might have streamed in from the old building's lobby. Half a dozen rooms lined the hallway, but a couple were empty. I mentally cataloged the sleeping patients as I walked down the hall.

The first was in for supplemental feeding by transfusion—a common geriatric need. The second patient had third degree sunburn after losing track of time at a college frat party. A third vampire had a persistent heartbeat that was mystifying our best cardiologist, and a fourth was recovering after a freak accident when she tripped while gardening night jasmine and nearly impaled her heart on a garden stake.

Nicholas Raines was in the last room on the right. I stood in his doorway, taking stock of the usual medical gear in the subdued glow of the nightlight. No heart monitor, of course, and no pulse ox. No respiration rate either. Vampire rooms were oddly peaceful in the midst of the usual hospital frenzy, especially in the hours before twilight.

"Hey, Doc."

I jumped at Raines's voice, but I managed to respond. "The sun hasn't set yet. You're supposed to be asleep."

He grunted—a sound that could have been agreement or rebellion. Then he said, "I didn't get your name last night."

"Ashley." Why did I say that? I never gave patients my first name. With exactly eleven months of career experience under my belt, I needed every possible tool for maintaining professional distance. I quickly added, "Ashley McDonnell. I'm the medical director here at Empire General."

"Then you can sign me out of this joint."

I walked over to his bed. His head was elevated, highlighting the rough stubble that shaded his jaw. A tangle of sheets and a soft cotton blanket wrapped around his waist. We gave bedding to transitioning vampires to make them feel comfortable. They certainly didn't need it for heat. "We'd like to keep you under observation for a couple of days."

His lips twisted inside the shadow of his beard. "First time you've seen a new vampire?"

"First time I've seen one who stays awake during the daytime."

He made a dismissive noise. "Mind over matter. Part of my job."

"Secret Service, right? You wear a suit and sunglasses and run beside the president's car?"

He shrugged. "Any chance I can get a doctor's note to explain why I missed roll call this morning?"

"Mr. Raines—"

"Nick."

I shouldn't have been so pleased by the confidence. Especially when I was about to give him devastating news. But that was part of a doctor's duty, helping patients adjust to changed circumstances. I took the approach I always did, making my voice firm, my words direct. "You aren't going to be a Secret Service agent anymore."

"Bullsh—, er, bullcrap," he said. I appreciated his making the vocabulary shift on the fly, even though I let fly with earthy words myself, now and then.

"Your present wakefulness aside, I'm afraid you're only working night shifts from here on out."

"There's no such thing as night-shift-only when your job is to protect the president."

"You don't have a choice." I nodded toward the painted-over window beside his bed. "I've seen vampires with third degree sunburns. It isn't pretty."

"I've never gotten by on my good looks." Belying his words, he lowered his chin, peering at me through eyelashes longer than any cold-blooded American male should be allowed. He added a slow grin, just enough to wreak havoc with my lady bits.

Yeah, I just called them lady bits. I was perfectly capable of giving a scientific description, but every woman in the world knew exactly what I was talking about.

"Sorry, big guy." I opted for keeping it light. "No can do."

His big fists released the tangle of sheets. I hadn't realized how tense he'd been.

"So, that's it, huh? The ER doc said I had to stay until my first meal. So, how long before I drink blood?"

"About a week. Your heart's stopped beating, and you aren't breathing anymore, but your body is still adjusting. Muscular changes take a few days. Nerves too. Don't be surprised if you're a little clumsy until your brain catches up. You can read all about it there." I pointed toward the Welcome the Night pamphlet prominently displayed by his bed.

Another snort of dismissal, followed by a feral grin. He didn't express his fangs, though. He probably hadn't realized he *had* fangs to express, but his intention was perfectly clear when he said, "Then I'll get the son of a bitch who did this to me."

I was a doctor. I wasn't supposed to root for bloody vengeance. But sweet Hecate, my aforementioned lady bits perked *right* up at the sound of Nick's determined growl. And they rolled over and begged for more when he ran a hand through his close-trimmed hair. "Sorry, Dr. McDonnell," he said. "You're not a vampire, are you?"

I shook my head, swallowing twice before I trusted my voice. "I'm a witch."

He laughed, then twisted his voice into a mincing register with a really bad British accent. "You'll turn me into a newt?"

I winced.

"Sorry," he said, his voice quickly restored to its customary rumble. "You must hear that a lot."

"Not as much as you'd think. I don't go around announcing my status to every person I meet." Sweet Hecate, I sounded more uptight than the proverbial schoolmarm. What *was* it with this guy? Everything he did set me off balance.

Like that teasing grin and the sudden look of speculation in his eyes. "So, work a spell for me."

A clammy blanket settled over my shoulders. "I can't."

He leaned closer. "Can't? Or won't?" I heard the steel beneath his words, a sudden intensity that made me pity the folks who got too close to the president on a rope line.

"Can't," I said shakily. Goosebumps rose on my arms, despite the fact that the hospital room was perfectly temperature controlled.

"Sorry, Doc." He leaned back against his pillows, actually sounding remorseful. "I didn't mean to push."

I scrambled for something safe to say. "We're not here to talk about me. We're supposed to concentrate on you. On helping you finish your transition."

He offered a winning smile. "Tell you what, Doc. I'll keep you posted on this whole transition thing, and you tell me what has you so terrified."

"I— I'm not terrified."

He merely stared at me, letting my lie shrivel between us.

"You're my *patient*!" My words might have been a little more forceful than necessary because I longed to accept his deal.

"I'll sign a waiver."

I forced myself to shake my head. To step back from his bed. To pin my gaze firmly on a point three inches from his grinning face. "I'll check in on you later tonight, Mr. Raines."

"Nick," he corrected. "And I'll look forward to that, Dr. McDonnell."

"Ashley," I said, just before I ducked out of his room, blushing seven different shades of red and cursing my stupid, treacherous lady bits.

5

"It's about time." Musker sauntered in from the bathroom as I sank into the chair behind my desk.

"Time for what?" I asked, tugging my white coat into place. The last thing I needed was my overly familiar familiar speculating about my non-existent love-life.

Musker's eyes rolled in a thoroughly disconcerting way that made me wonder if he was watching me or keeping an eye on my office door. "You don't have secrets from me."

Trying to smother a silent scream, I reached for my computer, determined to organize some files before the upcoming inspection.

"Don't bother," Musker said. "Becs is waiting for us."

"Waiting?" I asked, automatically extending an astral line to my warder.

Nothing.

I couldn't feel a hint of the bond that had connected me to Becs every single day for the past twelve years. And sitting there, probing the loss like a dental patient with a bad tooth, I couldn't say what frightened me more—dropping the connection or having been unaware of its absence for... Days? Weeks? Months?

How long had I been stripped of my magic?

Fighting a rising wave of panic, I gestured for Musker to lead the way. *He* had to know where Becs was. Sure enough, he skittered down the hospital's back staircase, heading for the basement. For the world's laziest familiar, he certainly managed to move quickly when the urge struck him. I didn't speak until we were sheltered behind the door of the hospital's largest storeroom.

"What are we doing here?" I whispered.

"Why are we whispering?" Becs asked in her normal voice.

I glanced at the ceiling. "The ER's up there. I figured we didn't want anyone overhearing our secrets."

Becs shrugged. "I just wanted to meet some place we wouldn't be interrupted. We've got some serious work to do."

"Work?"

For reply, she cast a quick look at my familiar. Musker gave his lips a quick lick before he said, "I did some research."

Musker usually only did things I directly ordered him to do—and then it took a minimum of three requests before I saw a glimmer of response. At his claim of initiative, a strange sense of foreboding stroked the nape of my neck. "What type of research?" I asked.

"I tapped into the familiars' network." He gave another one of those furtive eyerolls, this time splitting his attention between Becs and me. "I asked about witches who've lost their powers. Why. How long. And what they did to get them back."

A frozen brick settled in my belly. "Wh—" I had to clear my throat and start again. "What did you learn?"

Musker looked sideways at Becs. His tongue darted out again, a certain sign of his being nervous, and I half-expected him to scurry behind the boxes of surgical gloves. As it was, he knocked over a stack of votive candles, part of the esoteric equipment we kept on hand for our imperial patients. He hastily scooped the candles into a haphazard stack.

Even though each word iced my tongue, I forced myself to say, "Come on, Musker. What did you find out?" If I'd had any magical ability left, I would have pushed some witchy compulsion into the question.

His face was like a statue, every muscle carved from stone. The only movement I could see was his chest, rising and falling beneath his khaki shirt as he took breaths faster than any human could manage.

I forced myself to think like a doctor, one accustomed to delivering difficult diagnoses. My medical brain pushed words out of my mouth: "Is there a cure?"

Becs answered, and her voice was terrifyingly gentle. "If you had a little power left, you could create an anima, a spirit bound to your magic. You could set her to simple tasks, working basic spells to harvest her magic as your own."

I didn't have the first clue how to do that. Testing my nonexistent reservoir of magical power, though, I realized there was no sense in learning. I didn't have enough strength to make a bed, much less an anima.

I tried to keep my voice light. "So what's our next best option?"

Becs's fake smile was probably meant to give me comfort. It almost broke my heart. "Work the simplest spell you can think of. Even a tiny spark of magic will help reboot your powers."

Immediately, I plunged back to my first days at the magicarium. I'd sat in a room with seven other girls, each of us stationed behind a small white desk. The school days were long, sometimes eight, nine, even ten hours. We studied together constantly, took our meals at one long table, and slept in a dormitory every night.

Week after week, we tried to master the simplest spells. Our instructors lived and died by the Rota, lecturing that it was the best way to cement our powers, the most certain way to guarantee we would all reach our ultimate magical potential.

Even after we learned a spell, we were forced to repeat our

workings dozens of times, *hundreds* of times, the strongest among us rounding down her powers and the weakest stretching up.

Every word I'd ever learned at the magicarium was etched deep inside my brain.

I closed my eyes and offered myself to Hecate. I was supposed to feel the depths of her power, waiting to be channeled in whatever manner she allowed.

Terrified, I only felt empty.

But I was willing to pretend. I pointed a shaking finger at the closest votive candle and whispered:

"Dark shies,

Light vies.

Clear eyes,

Fire rise."

Nothing. No flash of darkness, no spark against a wick, no quick tongue of flame.

Musker produced a rowan wand from somewhere. Those pockets on his safari pants had to be good for something. "Try it again," he said, placing his fingers over mine as I gripped the length of wood.

"Dark shies,

Light vies.

Clear eyes,

Fire rise."

The candle simply sat there. But the rowan wand crumbled to dust.

Fighting my horror, I tried again, lining up a row of votives. I tried isolating one, in the center of the floor. I tried having Musker sit opposite me, letting him lean against my side, watching him crouch over the candle itself. Becs cast a protective circle, calling on the Guardians of Air and Fire, Water and Earth. I shouted the spell's words as loudly as I dared. I whispered them. I said them silently inside my head.

Nothing worked.

My powers were absolutely, completely, one hundred percent depleted.

"Enough," Becs finally said.

"What do we do now?" I barely recognized my voice, tiny and lost.

"We'll figure out something," Becs's tone was iron-hard with confidence.

"Like what?" I couldn't keep myself from pressing.

"I don't know," she finally admitted. But she added, "Yet."

She crossed the room and ushered us into the hallway. Before she closed the door, she took one more glance inside, making sure everything was back in place.

"Huh," she said, a wordless syllable of surprise as she darted back into the room. She bent down near the far wall and retrieved something that was almost invisible against the floor.

"What's that?" I asked,

She opened her fingers slowly, displaying her find. Stretched across her palm, yellowed and marked with a fine network of dark lines, was a delicate ivory comb. It was missing two teeth on one end and another in the middle.

I swallowed hard and met Becs's eyes. I didn't need magic to remember the encyclopedias I'd read about magical creatures. Neither did she. We spoke at the same time.

"Banshees."

6

I was a doctor. I was trained to respect life. I was supposed to accept my patients where I found them, healing those I could and offering comfort to those beyond my ability to help.

I. Hated. Banshees.

For one thing, no one knew exactly what the creatures were. The few people who'd lived after seeing one said they *looked* like ancient women, crones with withered faces and bedraggled hair. They wore tattered gowns that resembled torn and filthy grave-clothes. They rarely manifested in physical form; more often than not, only their faces appeared, contorted and screaming as they floated in mid-air.

Because they lacked a complete physical form, they often left behind combs as calling cards, dropping them from their straggling hair. Tortoiseshell or intricately worked silver or ivory—each banshee had her favorite adornment. As a witch learning about the spirits' existence, I'd wondered what a good haircut and some decent conditioner would do for them. Maybe the banshees could get a good night's sleep if they just managed a decent blow-out from a competent stylist.

Some people said banshees were fairies, descended from ancient British royalty. But fairies had no place in the Eastern Empire—the so-called "fair folk" had never crossed the ocean to the New World. If banshees were fae, they were different from every other type fairy ever recorded.

In the end, it didn't matter where they came from, even if they had royal blood. Banshees were simply loathsome creatures.

Their unearthly wails foreshadowed death in the next twenty-four hours.

Lovely.

I stared at the comb in Becs's hand as if it were a rattlesnake poised to bite. Forget inspection on Midsummer Eve. If the Eastern Empire Healthcare Facilities Accreditation Board knew we had banshees on the premises, they'd take away our charter faster than I could say "Hecate Preserve Us."

And I couldn't blame them.

I looked at my warder and said flatly, "Burn it."

"That won't change anything."

"I said *burn it*, Becs!"

She nodded somberly, slipping the comb into the pocket of her jeans to dispose of in short order.

I chewed on my lip. It didn't make sense, banshees terrorizing the hospital for no good reason. But sense or no, I had work to do —work that had been interrupted by Becs's unsuccessful suggestion that I try to regain my powers in the storeroom's privacy. I squared my shoulders and headed for the stairs.

"Where are you going?" Becs asked.

"Right now? I'm heading back to my office to work on getting this place ready for inspection."

Becs didn't contradict me. But she *did* cast a doubtful glance toward the votive candles on their shelf.

"Don't say it," I warned.

"I didn't say anything."

"But you're thinking very loudly."

She was my warder. She had my back. She'd never say out loud that a witch without powers—a mundane human woman—would never be allowed to run Empire General Hospital. We both knew the truth. Especially when that hospital had been visited by banshees.

7

For the next twenty-four hours, I prowled the corridors of Empire General, waiting to see which of my patients would die. I looked in on a nervous dryad so many times that she checked herself out of the hospital. Better to heal a canker on her own in the forest, than to submit to a crazy witch doctor in the city.

Responding to my repeated visits, the sole mother in our nursery—an ifrit with twins who were failing to thrive—sparked outrage so convincingly that I avoided the entire ground floor for the rest of the night.

The shifter ward was always a mixed bag. That night, we had a massively pregnant werecat in close quarters with two wolves who had been injured in a car crash, an alpha and his mate who could not consistently hold their human shape. A bear shifter rounded out the mix, lumbering up and down the hall, moaning in agony from an inflamed gall bladder, but refusing surgery for fear the organ would find its way onto the black market. After unsuccessfully ordering the wolves to stay in their rooms (a measure no alpha would tolerate), I resorted to giving the anxious werecat mother a fresh pillow filled with catnip.

Room by room, I checked on every creature under my care. Some cases were serious. Others were less critical. The one patient I wanted to visit—Nick—was strictly off limits; I didn't trust my judgment around him, not when I had a potential Code Blue on my hands.

Dawn came, and no one had died. Maybe the banshee had graduated bottom of her class in death prediction. Maybe the ivory comb had come from an absent-minded museum curator who happened to leave priceless ivory artifacts in random places.

Maybe the expected death just hadn't happened yet.

I made it through another twenty-four hours, subsisting on little more than coffee and catnaps. Shifters ward, elementals ward, ER, and witches—round after round after round. I added in the nursery when I thought I could get away with annoying the ifrit mother, and I checked on the first four rooms in the Vampire Unit three times during the night.

I avoided the end of the hallway. I avoided Nick.

As the third day started, I skipped right past caffeine and turned to amphetamines. Med school classmates swore by the little red pills. I'd never indulged—I'd always had my fatigue-banishing spells.

Becs caught me with my hand halfway to my mouth. "You'll end up with a killer headache."

"Thanks, Dr. Sartain."

She merely held out her hand. "Forget about the drugs. Take a nap for a few hours."

"I can't. My patients need me."

"Your patients have a dozen other doctors, ones who've slept enough to make reasonable medical decisions."

Tears sprang to my eyes. My own warder thought I was a crappy doctor.

Oh. My own warder thought I was too tired to act sanely.

"Go on, Ash. I'll get you if anything happens."

"But the banshee..."

"It's been two full days. It must have been a false alarm."

"Maybe she doesn't wear a watch."

"Ashley—"

"Okay," I said, because I really *was* exhausted, and I was enough of a doctor to know that I didn't want to start on the roller coaster of pharmaceutical uppers and downers. "But promise you'll wake me at noon."

"You need at least—"

"Promise!"

"Fine," she said, but I could see the words made her unhappy.

She *did* wake me at noon. But someone had engaged the tractor beam on my narrow bed. The mattress seemed to make my body heavier than a griffin's. I couldn't swing my legs over the side. I couldn't sit up straight. Instead, I punched my pillow and rolled over to face the wall. I was asleep before Becs shut my bedroom door.

The next time I woke, it was after dark. I scrambled to the bathroom and took care of pressing matters—brushing my teeth to eradicate a foul taste in my mouth, twisting my dirty hair into something resembling a messy bun, and only then tending to my complaining bladder. I topped a clean pair of scrubs with my omnipresent white coat, and I braced myself to face the hospital.

Shifters—fine.

Elementals—fine.

I descended to the second floor. Before I could check out the nursery, I heard a low voice teasing from the shadows: "There she is—the world-famous Dr. McDonnell herself."

I forced myself to turn around slowly, to have an easy smile on my face by the time I met Nick's gaze and countered, "If it isn't the world-famous Mr. Raines himself.

I didn't really carry it off. My voice quavered on his name. My body was far too eager to run toward him, no matter what my mind demanded. I compromised and *strolled* instead.

Apparently a gentleman, Nick stood as I approached. He'd

convinced someone to get him clothing beyond the usual hospital issue. Dark sweatpants hung low on his hips, and his black T-shirt was tight enough for me to examine his pecs for scars. Stubble was still deliciously dark on his face, and I wondered if he owned some special five-o-clock-shadow-producing razor.

"Wh—" I licked my lips. "What are you doing here?"

"I'm tired of staring at the same four walls. At least here I can see the sky and the stars." He gestured toward the windows that overlooked the back garden. "We vampires might Welcome the Night, but if I stare at the poster in my room for one more hour, I'm going to rip it to shreds."

I stiffened. "You're part of a very important pilot program—"

"Yeah, yeah, yeah. You're going to ensure a higher level of physical and mental health to the entire Eastern Empire by mindfully integrating new imperials into the existing Washington community, maintaining safe spaces and non-triggering interactions for all."

"You memorized all that?" I was shocked.

"I haven't had a hell of a lot else to do. After years of working for the Secret Service, night shift at the hospital is a little tame. Especially when the head honcho ignores you, night in and night out."

"I'm sorry," I said. "I was—"

"Protecting your patients against an imminent threat."

"How do *you* know that?"

"Rebecca Sartain stopped by. Professional courtesy, I guess. One lawman to another."

"Rebecca Sartain isn't a lawman. She's my personal warder."

"Same difference." He shrugged one lazy shoulder. I told myself not to watch the ripple of his abs. I ignored myself completely. "She seemed to think you might want my assistance in assessing a threat."

"The last thing I—"

He arched one eyebrow.

I hastily rephrased the lie I'd been about to tell him. "The last thing I want is for you—or Rebecca—to worry about patient care."

"She's got your back, Ashley."

He said my name, and my insides turned to caramel. I wanted to tell him I hadn't heard, just so he'd repeat himself. Instead I sank onto the upholstered couch. "She told you what happened? About the banshee?"

He nodded as he took one of the nearby chairs. I'd wanted him to sit beside me. From the tiny smirk on his face he knew that. His voice was serious, though, as he said, "I think you have to consider that someone planted the comb."

"But why put it in the *storeroom*? And in a dark corner? If someone wanted us to find the damned thing, they would have dropped it in a hallway."

"Maybe your banshee was stealing supplies. You might have interrupted her when the three of you began your impromptu little meeting."

"Becs told you about that?" I was incredulous. Our *impromptu little meeting* had been brought about my loss of the magic I'd known since birth. It was incredibly private, something that should have been kept secret from everyone.

But Becs had clearly trusted Nick enough to tell him. And she was the most close-mouthed person I'd met in my entire life. She'd still never told the secret about where we'd gone when I snuck out of the magicarium dorm on my birthday sophomore year, the night we— Yeah. She'd never told *that*.

Hulking in the shadows, Nick waited me out, giving me time to accept that my warder trusted him. He let me get used to the idea that I could trust him too. Maybe. Just a little.

I finally asked, "What supplies could a banshee possibly need?"

"New bandages to replace her torn ones?"

"Banshees aren't mummies!" I said, but I laughed.

"Are mummies real?" he asked. "I mean, not the kind you see in a museum, not old bones from ancient Egypt. Are real, living mummies wandering the streets of DC?"

The question proved he hadn't read all the materials from Welcome the Night, even if he'd memorized my mission statement. That was actually the whole idea behind the program—caring hospital staff were supposed to help newly turned vampires discover the reality of supernatural life in the Eastern Empire.

Well, I'd gotten off track when I was consumed with pursuing my banshee. But I was available to answer any and all patient questions, starting now.

"Mummies aren't real," I said. "But the rest of the old movies are pretty much on point. Vampires," I said, gesturing toward him. "The Wolfman."

"Tell me more about that." He leaned close enough that I caught a whiff of soap on his skin—not the industrial strength stuff we put in all the showers. Whoever had brought him clothes had made sure he smelled like pine trees.

I matched his posture, shifting forward until our knees almost touched. And I told him everything I knew about wolf shifters, dredging up details I thought I'd forgotten years ago. It was the least I could do, for a patient who'd been ignored for the better part of forty-eight hours.

And my tingling lady bits would settle for nothing less.

8

On Monday, I should have been getting ready for the inspection, but instead I taught Nick about modern witchcraft.

Physically, he was managing his transition just fine. But I could see the emotional strain as he reconciled himself to losing all of his former contacts. Most new vampires worried about family they'd never see again, about friends they'd lost. Nick never mentioned those, but he dropped longing references to his squad, the law enforcement colleagues he'd literally trusted with his life.

Who was I, to deny him a few hours of distraction when he asked about my imperial life?

We sat in my office, and I made Musker join us. I explained about familiars, about how they were bound into reliquaries, only to be released by a knowledgeable witch.

Trying to guess Musker's native species, Nick studied my familiar with an intensity that made me jealous. Musker, though, couldn't be bothered to respond. Instead, he blinked slowly, taking all the time in the world to tell me, "Go ahead, then. Tell him how you woke me."

I explained about how we witches centered our powers, offering up our thoughts and voices and hearts to Hecate. Then I recited the spell I'd used on Musker's reliquary years ago:

"Awaken now, scaled one, lizard of might.
Bring me your power, your strong second sight.
Hear that I call you and, willing, assist;
Lend me your magic and all that you wist."

Of course there wasn't any flash of darkness. I wasn't actually working any magic at all. But I remembered when my powers did work, and it ached to sense their absence, especially when I spent the rest of the night talking about my witchy sisters and all they could accomplish.

I waited until Nick headed upstairs, a scant five minutes before sunrise. Then, I turned to my familiar and said, "We've got to do something."

He yawned. "Sorry—that's not my thing at all. You go jump that vampire's bones by yourself. I'll just head back to the nap you interrupted."

"I don't want to jump—"

"Don't lie to your familiar." Musker rolled his neck, stretching every muscle and tendon. "A little somethin'-somethin' might be just the thing you need."

"You think *sex* will bring my powers back?"

"Not at all," Musker said. "But it might make you care less about losing them."

I gritted my teeth before I tried again, "We've got to do something a little more direct. Bring me my runes."

Musker stored the polished tiles in his sauna. We'd agreed that he could heat them against the in-floor coils and use them as hand-warmers on days he was feeling particularly sluggish. Which, of course, was just about every day.

The runes were made of granite, a stone that banished skepticism. They were inlaid with beryl, a crystal promoting clarity of thought. My hand-warmer ruse had a secret goal: I'd been trying to enhance my sluggish familiar's motivation. I was hoping the tiles' inherent powers would fire him up intellectually as well as physically.

Now, he fetched the stiff leather sack that protected my runes. When he deposited them on my desk, I expected to hear the clatter of stone against stone. The tiles, though, were oddly silent. I cast him an accusing glance, wondering what mischief his laziness had caused this time.

"I didn't do anything!" he protested.

"Exactly," I said, unable to keep a wry smile from my lips. Musker *never* did anything, if he could possibly help it.

Unlacing the bag, I prepared to do a simple spread—three randomly drawn tiles showing the past, the present, and the future. I couldn't ask for anything more basic. And maybe, just maybe, my powers might profit from the working.

I reached for the first tile, only to find the bag filled with dust. "Musker!" I yelped.

His tongue darted out, as if he tasted danger on the air. He took the bag from me and rolled the leather down, revealing the contents inside.

Every rune had crumbled. I was staring at a bag of grey powder, intermixed with a few swirls of blue-green crystals.

Immediately, I thought of the rowan wand Musker had given me in the storeroom. It, too, had crumbled to dust when I touched it.

I was clearly the destructive force in both these incidents. My loss of magic was extending to the tools I'd once used on a regular basis.

"You don't do anything by half measures, do you?" Musker asked.

"What's that supposed to mean?"

"When you lose your powers, you *really* lose them."

"Not helpful," I said.

He shivered, a slow trembling that rippled along his entire

spine. I wasn't sure if the motion was involuntary, or if he was trying to remind me that he'd rather be sleeping in his heated fortress. Maybe he was afraid that my failed magical attempts would consign him to the same pile of dust as my runes. Or, at the very least, that he'd be put back on the shelf at the magicarium, doomed to wait for some other naive witchling to awaken him.

"Go," I said, attempting to push down my despair. "We'll try something else tomorrow."

But when I crawled into my narrow bed, I couldn't think of anything else to try. Spells were just words, meaningless syllables strung together. The tools I'd mastered at the magicarium were literally dust.

I thought about sneaking downstairs. I could slip into Nick's room. I could crawl into his bed. Maybe Musker had been right—a little somethin'-something' *might* cure what ailed me.

But like it or not, Nick Raines was my patient, which made a relationship impossible.

And a part of me was afraid that if I touched him, he'd crumble away like my runes.

9

On Tuesday, I found Nick wandering in the garden, taking advantage of the light of a full moon to explore the property.

Okay, I didn't just happen to find him. I'd combed the entire hospital, increasingly worried that he'd checked himself out. A quick glance at his medical chart had warned that he was increasingly restless, probably due to his body's growing need to feed.

But I'd heard the longing in his voice when he talked about the Service. I knew he was mourning the professional life he'd left behind. And Empire General—even the gardens, with their summery flowers and fountains and perfect, hidden benches—was a pretty sorry substitute for being "Worthy of Trust and Confidence."

What? That was the Secret Service motto. I looked it up. I cared about my patient. Any responsible doctor would have done the same.

So, standing beside a koi-filled pond, I took Nick seriously when he asked me to distract him, to tell him more about his new imperial world. It seemed the perfect setting to tell him about elementals. We started with air spirits—sylphs like Dr. Hart. "It's always soothing to be around air elementals," I said. "Um, not to paint with too broad a brush."

He nodded, and I could almost imagine him taking notes. *Ifrits*, I pictured him writing as I went on. *Temperamental fire elementals capable of cleansing negativity and hatred. Sprites: Reclusive water elementals; the least likely to interact with other imperials.*

"And then there are the earth elementals," I said. "Gnomes."

"I guess you're not talking about little guys in the garden, the smiling ones with pointy red hats?"

I grimaced. "I wish. Gnomes are short, and they have beards —both men and women. But that's the end of any resemblance to kitschy backyard statues. Real gnomes are the shrewdest bankers in the empire, lending money at exorbitant rates. Most imperials want nothing to do with them, but they're the only source for moon-minted gold or fire-cut diamonds. If they had their way, entire blocks of DC would be converted to hoard-tunnels."

"Bastards," Nick said.

He was teasing me. But his tone was a reminder I wasn't supposed to play favorites among imperials. I rubbed my arms and said, "You can't be interested in all this."

"I'm interested in anything you want to teach me." Nick wasn't teasing anymore. At least, not in the poking-fun-and-maybe-making-me-laugh way. His voice had turned husky, barely loud enough to be heard over the trickling fountain at the far end of the pond. "I'm interested in you."

I felt myself blush as I muttered, "Don't say that."

"Why not?" he asked. Under the light of the full moon, his eyes were untroubled. "We're both adults, Ashley. We can talk about how we feel."

"I *feel* like you're my patient."

"Fine then. Here's a symptom for you to treat. I'm seeing things I've never seen before."

"That's your brain, accepting your new vampire senses."

"I'm hearing things too."

"It's the same thing. Your eyes, your ears—"

"I see the way your pupils dilate when you say you don't want anything to do with me." He took a single step closer. "And I just heard your pulse pick up."

"That's because you're standing in my space."

He took another step closer. "And now I can hear your breath catching in your throat."

"Th— That's because it's cold out here."

"I can hear you lie." He whispered those five words, so softly that *I* could barely hear them.

But he didn't step closer. He didn't close the gap between us. He stood there, perfectly still, his body already transformed by vampire blood so he could wait forever.

I was the one who moved. I moaned a little as I did, because I didn't trust myself, because I wanted him too much. His lips twisted into a smile the instant before I met them.

I knew his mouth would be cold. He was a vampire now, fully turned. But I'd read my books. I'd studied imperials. I knew he'd immediately absorb heat from my body; he'd take on the softness of my lips.

Nick Raines knew how to kiss. For just a heartbeat, my doctor-brain cataloged what he was doing—that was my caninus muscle and my buccinator muscle and sweet Hecate what was he doing to my orbicularis oris?

But then my brain stopped managing things, and my body took over. I leaned into his strength. I felt his hands spread wide across my back.

I kissed him until my head buzzed, until I was starved for air, starved for more. I had to pull back, had to raise trembling fingers to my lips.

"So, Doc?" Nick said. "Got a diagnosis?"

"You're incorrigible."

"Only when I have the right inspiration."

"Nick..." I said. *Nick, I can't do this. Nick, I'm dealing with too many other crises—the hospital inspection, and my lost powers, and the banshee premonition... Nick, I want to rip off your clothes right here in the light of the full moon and do things so dirty I don't even know what to call them.*

He couldn't hear that. I didn't say any of that out loud.

But he nodded as if I'd poured my heart out. He brushed his fingertips against my cheek. He slipped an errant lock of hair behind my ear.

"Go on," he said. "I'm staying outside for a few more hours."

I wanted to stay. I needed to go.

My orbicularis oris protested, but I headed back to the hospital. Alone.

10

I stopped in the kitchen, desperate for something to calm my mind, to stop the spinning images of what Nick and I had just done, of all the things I wished we'd done Opening the pantry, I reached for the familiar bags of Red Rose tea.

But then my eyes fell on Natasha's stash of herbs. Some were meant for flavor, of course, but others were intended to treat imperial patients. I'd studied herbcraft for years at the magicarium. I recognized everything on the shelves.

Cinnamon.

Cloves.

Thistle.

Those were all linked to Fire, tied to the elementals of the southern quadrant when I worked a ritual. Ever since I'd lost my powers, I'd been focusing on fire, on my basic schoolgirl spell to light a candle. Maybe I just needed to supplement my magical base, feed the fire within me.

Before I could talk myself out of it, I filled a saucepan with water. The gas flame whooshed to life, presaging the spell I hoped to work.

Impatiently, I waited for the water to boil. I had no idea how much of the herbs to add. I tossed in three curling sticks of cinnamon bark and an entire handful of cloves. I sifted dried thistle flowers over all of it, enough to cover the water's surface.

I turned off the burner and let my tea steep. I wasn't following a rule book. I wasn't working through a lesson I'd mastered years before. I was doing what felt right, what felt honest and good.

My lips still tingled from the touch of Nick's scruffy beard. I could remember the weight of his hands on my back and the strange flipping tension below my waist as he sent me back inside the building. I still felt the struggle between what I wanted to do and what I knew was right.

My fire tea was ready.

I found a sturdy stoneware mug, one of the plain white ones that the hospital bought by the gross. Pouring through a strainer, I caught the fragrant herbs and set them in the sink.

The tea smelled familiar—cinnamon and cloves like the coffee cake my grandmother baked when I was a child. But it smelled strange as well—a scent I thought of as "green", like cucumber or celery. Or thistle.

I blew gently on the cup, breathing in the steam. Could my problem be solved so easily? Could I drink an herbal potion and restore my missing magic?

I gulped a healthy swallow, letting the hot liquid wash over my tongue and coat the back of my throat. It was strong—stronger than any black tea—and it was warming and nourishing and good.

I opened the drawer to the left of the walk-in refrigerator. Sure enough, in a jumble of string and notepads and pencils and pens was a box of birthday candles. I'd bought them myself, putting one on a cupcake for Dr. Hart's recent birthday. Increasing staff morale, I'd told myself. Making everyone feel part of a family.

My fingers shook as I took out a blue-and-white-striped candle. I stared at it, unblinking, thinking about the taste of the tea, the heat of the herbs as I swallowed, the essential element of fire. I'd consumed the potential of those herbs. I'd fortified myself to work my spell. I'd thought outside the box of the magicarium's oldest lessons, and now I was ready to reap the benefit of my creativity.

My voice trembled as I spoke the familiar words.

"Dark shies,
Light vies.
Clear eyes,
Fire rise."

Nothing.

No burst of fire. No ripple of light. Not even a tiny spark of heat.

I'd been so certain. So sure. I thought I'd finally found a way past the block on my powers, through the disaster I'd brought upon myself. I was too stunned to cry as I poured the dregs of my tea down the drain. Instead, I double-checked that I'd turned off the burner, and I headed up the stairs.

But I didn't fall asleep until the sun was high in the sky.

11

I woke up shortly after noon. It was Wednesday, the one day off I was guaranteed by contract. Not that a contract would mean anything if yet another disaster struck Empire General. For now, though, I was off-duty, and I intended to luxuriate in a little quiet time.

Lying in bed, I replayed everything that had happened the night before. I knew I should feel bad about letting things go as far as they had with Nick, but I couldn't summon any remorse.

In fact, I started to argue that he wasn't actually *my* patient; Dr. Hart was in charge of his case. And I was pretty sure Nick wasn't a babe in the woods when it came to relationships. If that kiss was any indication, he was an awful lot more experienced than I was, my first time with Caden "Speedy" Park notwithstanding.

In any case, Nick would be discharged tonight, as soon as he'd fed from a qualified Source. After that first meal, there'd be no reason—physical or mental—to keep him on the vampire ward.

Of course, all that justification didn't solve my other problems. I was fresh out of ideas for how to jumpstart my magical abilities. I'd tried spells. I'd tried using a wand and runes. I'd tried a potion.

I was terrified to pick up any grimoire, for fear the book would be destroyed by my touch. I couldn't raid my stash of witchy implements, lest I ruin my most precious arcana. I didn't dare reach out to any other Washington Coven witch, because I might spread my predicament.

I was absolutely, one hundred percent alone. Well, except for Musker and Becs. But if either of them had known a cure, they would have told me days earlier.

As the sun slanted through my curtains, my mind twisted around on itself—back to Nick and that kiss—That! Kiss!—and his imminent release from the hospital and the pending inspection and my missing powers, and, and, and...

I needed to break the cycle.

I dug out a running bra and an old Georgetown T-shirt. I found shorts at the back of the armoire. I got down on my hands and knees, scrambling halfway beneath my bed before I located both of my running shoes. Clean socks, a high ponytail, five minutes of stretches, and I was ready to hit the trail.

I'd never win any prizes for speed—after jogging the first mile, I slowed to a determined walk. Nevertheless, I had the endurance of a pack mule. I climbed Capitol Hill, conscious of every step pulling on my tight hamstrings. I took to the National Mall like an indefatigable tourist. I passed the architectural blight of the World War II Memorial and skirted the raw black wound of the Vietnam Veterans Memorial.

The sun swept across the sky to the west. Exhausted tourist families shuffled to subway stations, hot and dusty after long days of sightseeing. Commuters filled the roads and bridges, streaming toward their homes.

I'd always liked Memorial Bridge, with its pedestrian sidewalks and its view of Arlington Cemetery. Now, my odyssey took me over those grassy hills. I chided myself when my mind tried to circle back on my dilemmas at the hospital. I sought distraction by counting row after row of gravestones, marker after white marble marker.

Each step erased a little tension from my body, smoothing over a protest in my mind. I was quiet. I was empty. I was clear.

Finally, I stood on the portico of Arlington House, in the heart of the national cemetery. My legs trembled a little, finally complaining about the distance I'd traveled. I noted the spasms with the dispassion of a clinician, just as I would have recorded my respiration rate and pulse on a hospital chart.

At my feet, close by the right toe of my running shoes, spread a dandelion, its sharp-toothed leaves as broad as my thumb. A stalk rose up with a tight-furled flower, barely hinting at yellow across the top.

I could open that flower with magic. I could expose it to the soft evening air.

I didn't allow myself to think. I didn't draw on formal words, on any spell I'd ever mastered while sitting in a classroom or reading from a book. I didn't even make a formal offering of my thoughts, my voice, and my heart; instead, I just opened myself to Hecate, to her terrible love and understanding.

Grow, I thought toward the bud.

I poured all my concentration into the single syllable. I imagined the green husk opening, the damp yellow spikes unfurling in the dusk.

Grow, I thought again.

The stalk would bend just a little, curving with the weight of the new flower. Somewhere in the dirt below, the roots might shift, maybe a hundredth of an inch.

Grow! I pleaded.

But the tight-wrapped bud didn't waver.

Suddenly I saw myself, sweaty and exhausted, hunched over a

weed in the middle of a field of gravestones. I'd lost it. I'd well and truly lost it.

How had I ever thought this would work, anyway? No one at the magicarium had ever suggested that physical exhaustion was a path to magical enlightenment. No one had ever taught us about emptying our minds. What made me think I knew more than all the magisters who had conducted my training?

My mother was right. I never should have wasted my time and effort and energy with medical school, especially not with the intention of treating imperials. I didn't know enough to complete a one-word working. I could never be suited to run Empire General.

Blinking back tears, I stared out at the horizon. DC was swaddled in twilight—the ghostly white marble of the Lincoln Memorial and the Washington Monument and the purple-toned water of the Reflecting Pool. The National Mall's grass looked black in the darkness, setting off the Capitol's titanium glow. The moon was rising, one night past full.

I couldn't see Empire General from here; it was hidden behind the dark green of the Library of Congress's dome. I couldn't see it, but I knew it was there—offering medical care to assorted imperials, providing jobs to hardworking staff, and serving as my home, at least for another three weeks. After that, after we failed the inspection, everyone would be turned out. No over-arching medical care. No paycheck signed by the Eastern Empire. And definitely no bedroom in the attic.

I had nowhere else to go.

I thought about calling an Uber. I could even hail one of DC's ubiquitous taxis. But I took grim comfort in the ache of my body —it was real and it would last, even after I lost everything else I valued.

The bells on some church tolled nine as I pushed my way through the iron gate on Empire General's front lawn. I took care to close the latch behind me, tugging it twice, even though anyone could reach through the bars and grant themselves easy access. I took my time walking up the path, studying the grass growing between the flagstones. A tiny dandelion nestled beside the walk, its yellow flower bleached by moonlight.

If I hadn't been staring at the flower, I probably would have seen the shadow detach itself from the porch. I would have noted the broad shoulders, the lean height. I would have seen the face, still bristled but flushed with new blood.

As it was, I shrieked like a terrified mouse when Nick called my name.

"Sorry," he said, his lips curling in a wry smile. "I thought you knew I was here."

I shook my head. "I was...thinking about something else."

"So I gathered."

I stepped back to get a better look at him. "You fed."

"From a qualified Source. Just like the handbook says."

"And?"

His fingers folded into fists, squeezed, and released. "I feel good. Strong. Like none of this ever happened, and I'm a regular guy again."

"Post-prandial euphoria. It's a documented effect."

"Thanks, Doc. I read about that." His eyes glinted in the moonlight, softening his mocking tone. "You look like you could use a feeding yourself."

I wasn't hungry until he said the words. But suddenly, my mouth watered. My belly twisted, offering an embarrassing growl.

He laughed. "Come on," he said, offering me his hand as I climbed up the steps.

I didn't think I'd need the assistance, but my quads said otherwise. Shivering in the hospital's dim lobby, I followed Nick back to the kitchen.

"Hey," I protested half-heartedly. "Patients aren't allowed back here."

"I'm not a patient," he said. "I signed myself out after I fed."

"Then why were you—"

"I was waiting for you. All those book smarts, Doc, and you couldn't figure that out?"

I stared as he tugged open the walk-in refrigerator's heavy door. He studied the shelves with an appraising eye before he collected a flat of eggs and a side of bacon, butter and cream and a full loaf of bread. Back in the kitchen, he plucked a skillet from the pot rack, and he rummaged for a whisk.

"You *cook*?" I asked, even as my stomach urged me to crunch through half a dozen raw eggs.

"No one else feeds me. Not with the crazy hours I keep."

Fed. Kept. But I didn't correct him. I was too busy watching the tattoos ripple on his forearms as he cracked three eggs into a bowl, tapping each against the countertop to maximize efficiency.

In minutes, I was sitting down to a late-night feast—eggs and bacon and toast, all washed down with cream-spiked coffee. I ate every bite, mopping the plate clean with my last bite of toast. I should have been self-conscious with Nick watching me, his eyes following every bite I raised to my lips. But I was too hungry to care. I needed to feed my body, needed to replenish the energy I'd wasted on my marathon walk.

I only spoke when Nick refilled my mug. "I can't," I said. "I'll never get to sleep if I drink that."

His eyes met mine over the cup. "Actually, that was my plan."

His tone left no doubt as to how he thought I should fill my insomniac hours. "Nick—"

"Stop," he ordered, setting down the carafe to emphasize his command. "You never were my doctor. And I'm not a patient anymore."

"I— I'm not interested."

"The hell you aren't." He planted his hands on the table. "I'm a vampire, Ashley. I've got superior eyesight and hearing and I can smell—"

Now it was my turn to say, "Stop!"

But I was a doctor. I knew that everything he said was true. And indelicate as his words might be, my entire body was casting a quite enthusiastic vote in this unexpected election.

Even that wasn't true. Nothing about this encounter was *unexpected*. I'd been drawn to Nick from the moment he rampaged through my ER. He'd made no secret that he felt the same.

I put my napkin on the table. I pushed back my chair. I took three steps, four, until I stood directly in front of the most attractive vampire—the most attractive *man*—I'd ever met in my life.

I felt the heat of his recent feeding through my fingers on his shoulders, through my palm on his chest after he stood. His arms still broadcast residual heat as they folded around me, as he pulled me close in an iron-clad embrace.

I wanted this. I needed this. I leaned my head back, purposely exposing the length of my neck. I felt him grow hard against me.

"Ashley," he growled, but I kissed him to stop him from saying anything more. His fangs sprang into action; I felt them slide against my lips.

He froze for nearly a minute, startled or longing or something else. He mastered his transformed body, though, controlling his vampire instincts. He absorbed his fangs and traced the tip of his tongue along the sensitive path from my ear to my carotid.

Then *I* was the one who said *his* name. And I was the one who took his hand. And I was the one who led the way upstairs, down the hall, into my narrow bedroom with its tiny bed shoved beneath the window.

My doctor-brain reminded me we didn't need to scare up condoms. He couldn't make me pregnant, and his vampire body was impervious to disease.

Instead, we could focus on more important problems. Nick pulled my mattress onto the floor. I showed some ingenuity in stripping off fabric—the top-sheet that formed an unnecessary tangle, his clothes, mine.

And then we worked together, hard work, work that left us laughing and breathless and begging for more. A whole lot more.

Three times more before dawn, in fact.

12

I woke hours later, momentarily confused about why the ceiling was so far away, about why every muscle in my body ached, about why a man's heavy arm was curled across my body, pulling my spine close against his hard, sculpted chest. I could just make out the ink on that arm, the five-pointed star and blue-and-red shield, with numbers swirled beneath, like some sort of date.

I squinted to make out those numbers in the dim grey light.

I shouldn't be able to see the numbers at all. My room should be pitch dark.

"Nick!" I shoved hard against his arm.

"Mmm." He rolled over on his back, doing his best to take me with him.

"The sun is almost up!"

His grin was lazier than anything I'd ever seen on Musker's face. Despite his indolence, his fingers began to explore my legs, starting with the sensitive hollow behind my left knee. "Jesus, woman," he muttered, eyes still closed. "You're insatiable."

I pulled away, scrambling for one of the sheets I'd discarded the night before. At the same time, I planted the soles of my cold feet against Nick's taut abs. A fat lot of good that did. His skin was cooler than mine.

"Come on, Nick. You can spend the day in your room downstairs."

He was halfway asleep again. "Not a patient anymore," he slurred.

"You will be, if you don't get some place safe before the sun rises. There are a couple of empty rooms on the ward."

He grumbled, but he lurched to his feet. He could have pulled his clothes on faster. He definitely didn't need to flex his arms *that* much as he tugged his T-shirt over his head. And oh, sweet Hecate, he didn't need to run a hand over his bristled jaw as he gave me that devilish grin.

"Come tuck me in," he said.

"Go," I ordered, because I was sorely tempted.

He did, but not before pulling me close for a bruising kiss. I gasped as his fangs expressed, but he merely traced the line of my jugular, not coming close to drawing blood. It took every last shred of my devastated will-power to push him out the door and then I turned the deadbolt behind him—for both our sakes.

I took my time getting dressed, starting with a long, hot shower. I shampooed my hair twice. I applied lotion to my elbows and my feet. I took extra care with my foundation and blush, with eyeliner and mascara, with lipstick on my swollen lips.

I couldn't stop smiling.

I found a long-forgotten dress at the very back of my armoire, a timeless sheath of blue cotton. I'd worn it once, attending Easter brunch at my mother's house. She'd disapproved because it showed off my arms. She hadn't liked my slingback sandals either. Well, Mother wasn't visiting Empire General today.

Humming a tuneless song, I selected dangling earrings, ones fashioned from sodalite. I might not be able to focus my powers through the stones, but I could remember the confidence they inspired. Besides, I wasn't about to use my fall-back silver hoops.

Not when there was a chance I might accidentally scald a vampire.

I'd just finished brushing my hair when the air shimmered in front of me. I took a step back, nearly falling when my heels sank into the mattress on the floor. Before I could shriek in surprise, Becs materialized in the center of the room.

My warder barely glanced at the chaos of my love nest. She was already grabbing my wrist, steadying my weight and pulling me forward. Her palms cupped my shoulders, and I felt the stomach-lurching pressure of *reaching* to a new destination, fully under my warder's power.

She kept me safe upon our arrival, of course. She always did. Even as my ears registered the chaos of hysterical sobbing, even as my eyes took in the arched windows of the elementals ward on the hospital's second floor, Becs shoved me behind her lithe back. Her curved blade of blue steel sparked dangerously as I tried to decipher exactly what was going on.

"I won't stay," a dryad shouted, her voice trembling like leaves in a gale. "I'd rather take my chance with oak wilt."

"You aren't being reasonable," Dr. Blanchard protested. The undine in charge of care for all elementals applied her most soothing voice, as if she could wash away her patient's terror with simple conviction. "Wilt can have disastrous long-term effects if not properly treated."

"Death has longer term effects," the dryad snapped. She tried to tear off her hospital bracelet, but she couldn't defeat the plasticized loop. "I'll send someone for my things." She flounced down the hallway before Dr. Blanchard could summon another argument.

"She's not the only one," a sprite spluttered, using the tentacles of his native form to split his own hospital bracelet. A naiad chimed in, along with two ifrit, all of them creating a cacophonous symphony of protest.

"Please," Dr. Blanchard burbled, her words washed away

before they could have any effect. "Please," she repeated before a sylph rushed down the hallway, knocking over a wheelchair as he chose the straightest line to the stairs.

"Stop!" I shouted, projecting from the bottom of my rib-cage. "What in the name of Hecate is going on here?"

They all started talking at once—every one of the elementals. "No!" I snapped. "Dr. Blanchard! Tell me exactly what happened."

The undine blinked vaguely, but she raised her voice enough to be heard over the resentful shifting of our patients. "I'd just finished morning rounds when I saw it."

"It?"

Dr. Blanchard swallowed hard, craning her neck as if she needed to drive a bad taste out of her mouth. It took every fiber of her limited courage, but she managed to say, "A shuck."

My throat locked. Now that I knew what to look for, the signs of the hellhound were obvious. Claw marks stood out on the linoleum floor, deep scratches where fiery paws had scrabbled for purchase. Scorch marks blackened each doorframe on the hallway, clear evidence that the harbinger of death had peered in at patients. I could picture his fiery eyes, blazing bright even in daylight.

Sweet Hecate, no wonder the ward was freaking out. The shuck had just announced the imminent death of every person on the unit.

"B— Becs?" I finally asked. My warder had finished her own initial surveillance, sword at the ready as she verified that no shoulder-high, flame-eyed, fire-breathing black dogs remained on the premises.

She turned to me like a soldier reporting disastrous defeat on a battlefield. "It's gone," she said.

"How the hell did it get in here?" I asked, terror melting to anger in the aftermath of adrenaline. "Where's hospital security?"

My warder sheathed her sword in the ether, as if her decisive motion could possibly calm me. Her voice was level as she said, "Jerome called me when he realized he needed backup."

"Backup? Where's Mikaela?"

Becs looked meaningfully at the claw marks scratched into the floor. "No centaur in history would face down a shuck," she said.

Of course they wouldn't. Centaurs, for all their human tempering, were essentially prey animals. It was something of a miracle Mikaela had lasted as a security guard this long.

"Where's Jerome now?"

Becs gestured toward the window. "He chased the shuck away."

I tried to picture our geriatric gargoyle trailing after a fire-breathing hell-hound. At least Jerome was relatively inured to flame. And the beast would likely take to ground quickly, unwilling to risk discovery by any human in the vicinity.

"Excuse me." An ifrit shouldered past me with surprising force. On the surface, her two words were polite, but even a stone-deaf gorgon could have heard the fury beneath them. Her aged face was framed by curling grey hair and wisps of smoke rose from her skull, a clear sign that she was barely containing her rage.

"Ms. Nar," I said. "If you'll just step back into your room, we'll have this taken care of in no time."

"I'm not stepping back anywhere," the fire elemental said. "I may have cataracts, but even *I* can see where a hellhound has walked."

"Please, Ms. Nar—"

"Don't *please* me. I knew this was a bad idea from the moment my son suggested it."

Cataract surgery was always risky for ifrits. Their fire-based metabolism offered exceptional risk to the eye's delicate organs. That was why Layla Nar had been scheduled for an in-patient procedure.

Before I could make her change her mind, a sylph hurtled by. "Makani!" I cried out in surprise. I should have been more formal, but the wind spirit was a long-time friend. We'd met at Georgetown, where the Hawaiian elemental had come to study international relations.

Apparently, she wasn't feeling diplomatic this morning. "Get out of my way," she said. "Forget that gastric sleeve. I'll take my chances being fat."

Within minutes, the ward was empty. We wouldn't be doing any knee replacements on undines. The discreet tummy tuck we'd planned for a sprite was scuttled. Our first-ever hysterectomy for a nephele was history.

In short, every elective procedure scheduled for Empire General's elementals was canceled.

I wanted to say they were being absurd. They were taking more risks postponing their surgeries than if they'd had them as planned. But Hippocrates's old oath reared its annoying head.

First do no harm.

Could I really say no harm would come to my patients when a hellhound had stalked the ward?

I ordered the nurses to help with the mass exodus. Becs, though, defied me directly, refusing to keep watch over the departures. Instead, she stayed by my side in case the shuck returned.

Stalking back toward my office, I found Mikaela crouching behind the security desk. Even across the lobby, I could see the twitch beneath her left eye. Her fingers were so clumsy on the keyboard she was attacking that I was certain she was typing gibberish.

When she saw me, her long face drooped into a frown. "I shouldn't have left the ward, Dr. McDonnell. I know that." She shuddered, a rolling tic that cascaded down her entire body.

"At least you called Ms. Sartain before you left." I nodded toward Becs, hoping my warder's presence would sooth the spooked centaur. Then I said, "Call Imperial Staffing. See if they can send a couple of giants to cover though the weekend."

The extra staff would leave a gouge in my budget as deep as the hellhound's claw marks upstairs. But I didn't have any alternative. I had to keep my remaining patients and staff safe.

Mikaela nodded and reached for her phone.

Becs followed me into my office, waiting until I'd closed the door before she asked, "You think this will all blow over by Monday?"

I shook my head. "I'm almost certain it won't. But the temps will give us time to figure out what we really need to do."

If every one of my patients checked out, my problem would go away. So would my job, of course—and deservedly so. I'd been primping and preening after a night of wild vampire sex, instead of paying attention to a soul-crushing threat on my doorstep.

For the first time since I'd opened the accreditation board's letter, I wondered if it was worthwhile to fight for Empire General.

Maybe we'd all be better off with the hospital closed.

13

The giants arrived by noon. Even though the elementals ward cleared, most other patients stayed put. Some, of course, had no choice—not every procedure at Empire General was elective.

I stalked the hallways, obsessively tallying the number of occupied beds throughout the hospital. I only forbade myself to enter the vampire ward. A tiny, illogical corner of my mind worried that I'd wake Nick, that the power of my emotions would force him from the safety of his vampire-bound sleep even though the sun was still high in the sky.

Ultimately, I let Becs lure me out of the office. She insisted that I had to eat lunch anyway, and the new security guards had everything under control. I let her *reach* both of us to a familiar park bench, looking out at the Potomac River in the heart of Georgetown. I couldn't count the number of times I'd walked down the hill as a med student, seeking a break from intractable classes. Staring out at the slow-flowing water, I could feel my blood pressure return to normal.

Becs dug into her backpack and produced a pair of waxed-paper-wrapped sandwiches. She passed me mine—roast beef and brie on sourdough with a double serving of thin-sliced cucumber, just the way I liked it. I could even forgive the, um, aroma of her egg salad on rye because she took such good care of me.

"This is amazing," I said, after I'd swallowed the first perfect bite. I couldn't believe she'd pulled together such fare from Natasha's kitchen.

"When was the last time you ate?"

"Last night!" I said defensively.

"I meant food," she said, arching her eyebrows in deliberate provocation.

I blushed, but I said self-righteously, "I meant food, too. I had bacon and eggs and toast!" At her skeptical look, I became fascinated by the crust of my sandwich. "Nick made it for me, when I came back from my walk."

"I want to know about that walk," she said. "But first tell me about Nick."

He's different from any guy I've ever met. He makes me feel safe, even when everything is crazy. He doesn't care if I've lost my powers.

I shrugged. "He's a guy."

Becs put her sandwich in her lap. "Here, I'll make this easier for you. He's hotter than an ifrit in Phoenix. But you've had your pick of hot guys before."

"Yeah, right."

"I'm serious," she insisted. "You could have gone out with half my senior class at the Academy, if you'd ever opened your eyes to see they existed. And you had your pick in college school too. There were even a couple of med students worth a night or two."

I snorted. "I didn't exactly have time for a boyfriend then."

"That's my point. You didn't then, and you don't now. But you seem to have chosen one, all the same. And he's a vampire."

"What?" I asked, pretending to be shocked.

Becs didn't let me off the hook. "Come on, Ash. You know that complicates things. The day/night schedule alone is a killer. What's going on?"

I shrugged. "I'm just having fun. It's not like I'm going to hold out for my One True Love. It's absurd to wait for the Promised One when he could be ten thousand miles away, working in a call center in Hyderabad."

"But..." Becs prompted when I ran out of steam.

"But there's something special about Nick. I... I like the person I am when I'm with him. Does that make sense?"

She nodded. "It makes a lot of sense. So long as you remember that you've only just met him."

A sliver of ice cut through the sunny afternoon. "What do you mean by that?"

"I mean, he showed up right before things started getting crazy at the hospital."

"Things have always been crazy at the hospital."

"You know what I mean," she reprimanded. "We never had banshees before Nick came around. Shucks, either."

The sliver of ice turned into a glacier calving across my heart. "You think he's going to *kill* someone?"

"I don't know what to think." She was using her warder voice —calm, implacable, utterly without emotional content. They must have taught an entire course at the warder's Academy about using that tone.

"Wait a second. *You're* the one who told *him* about our meeting in the storeroom."

My protest made me remember the banshee whose comb we'd found in broad daylight. And the hellhound who'd attacked that morning had only made its appearance after I hustled Nick into seclusion for the day.

"He couldn't have let either one of them in," I said, hating the defensive note in my voice.

"I'm not saying he did. But we never had a problem with harbingers of death before Nick showed up."

I couldn't deny that. But I also couldn't believe Nick had anything to do with my ongoing problems at the hospital. I would have *felt* something when I was with him—something off—if he was essentially a terrorist working for some huge, dark, unknown cause. That type of evil would be evident even *if* my powers were on the blink. Right?

I offered up a prayer to Hecate that denial was just a river in Egypt. If I was wrong, the Empire Bureau of Investigation would end up in permanent residence on the hospital grounds. And I could very well find myself in a permanent cell, far beneath the Eastern Empire Night Court.

I folded wax paper over my sandwich. I'd lost my appetite. "Whatever happens, I know you'll keep me safe," I finally said.

"Of course I will." Becs made it sound as if no sane person could ever doubt any alternative. But then she ruined everything by saying, "Physically. I'll die before anyone hurts you physically."

Great. That meant she thought Nick was going to break my heart.

I couldn't imagine she was right. And even if she was, I couldn't imagine not taking the chance. I had it bad for my shadowy vampire...lover? Boyfriend? Whatever.

Becs finished her sandwich as if we'd talked about nothing more disturbing than the Nationals' chances in the post-season. Then, she reached into her backpack, producing a pasteboard box with a familiar gold sticker.

"Friends?" she asked, passing the treasure to me.

"For Cake Walk cupcakes?" I asked. "You're stuck with me forever."

She laughed as I sliced a fingernail through the paper label. I knew what I'd find before I opened the box: Three miniature Caramel Castle cupcakes—each one consisting of four layers of yellow cake secured by caramel icing--and three Lemon Leaps—sweet lemon cake with sour lemon curd, finished off with sugared lemon rind. Becs was the safe, secure Castle, while I took the Leaps. That's the way our friendship had always been.

She waited until I'd eaten two of mine, devouring each in a pair of bites. Then she said, "I have a suggestion, but you're not going to like it."

I looked at her warily. "Suggest away."

"We need help with security at the hospital."

"You saw those giants!"

She nodded. "And they'll be great, through the weekend. But you said yourself we need a more permanent solution."

I frowned. With a theft, a banshee, and a hellhound in little more than a week, "solutions" were thin on the ground.

Becs obviously took my silence as permission to continue. "Empire General has to accommodate everyone. You have to secure the building against every type of imperial, no exceptions."

"That's in our charter—we're required to treat every denizen of the Eastern Empire."

"The only other institution I can think of with such a diverse population is the night court. They're required to hear every case in the Eastern Empire." She paused until I nodded, and then she said, "The court had to work out a massive security scheme—maybe even more than you do, because they've got mundanes going in and out of the same building."

"So if we talk to the court about their security..."

"...We might get a handle on what we *should* be doing," she confirmed.

It felt like failure to reach outside the hospital. But I didn't want to feel this lost for even one day more. "Who's in charge of security for the night court?" I asked.

"A vampire. His name is James Morton."

A vampire. Unbidden, I remembered the feel of Nick's fang alongside my jugular.

Silently ordering my imagination to settle down, I said, "Can you set up a meeting?"

"I'll go over there tonight."

"Perfect," I said.

"But I have one requirement."

"This is the part I'm not going to like."

She had the guts to meet my gaze. "I don't want Nick Raines knowing about it."

My initial response was to protest. Nick had done nothing but stand by me. He'd made me dinner. He'd kept me safe.

But Becs had made a hell of a lot of dinners for me over the years. And she'd raised her sword in my defense—against threats real and imagined—more times than I could count.

She was my best friend. She was my warder. She deserved one favor, even one that made me feel like a traitor to the man I'd slept with just the night before.

"Okay," I said. "Set something up."

"And?" she pressed.

I hated the words, but I said them. "And I won't tell Nick."

"Thank you," Becs said quietly.

"You're wrong," I warned her.

"I can't tell you how much I want that to be the case."

We sat on the bench for a long time after that, watching the river flow slowly downstream. Ultimately, we ate our last two cupcakes, but the lemon rind left a bitter aftertaste that no amount of water could wash away.

14

It turned out, the Eastern Empire District Court was wrapped up in some sort of trial of the century, a vampire kingpin who'd slipped out of court custody several times before. James Morton refused to meet until the following week, and then he told us he could only spare half an hour.

Becs agreed. Half an hour was better than none.

That left me with a week of fretting.

I should be preparing for the Midsummer Eve inspection. Frankly, though, that felt like an insurmountable barrier. I mean, what sort of examining board would approve an institution run by a witch with no powers, where valuable drugs disappeared without a clue, and banshees and hellhounds roamed the premises?

I was doomed. But Nick was doing his best to make me forget my imminent demise. And keeping me from getting to work on the resumés I should be distributing far and wide to human hospitals.

"What do you do for fun?" he asked me on Friday night, a couple of hours after I learned James Morton was placing us in a holding pattern.

"Fun?"

"Maybe we could go out to dinner? Play gin rummy? Fu—, er, screw like rabid mongeese?"

I laughed. "Isn't that mongooses?"

"So just to be clear—you don't have a problem with the concept, just the vocabulary?"

"Um, let's start with dinner."

"And then?" he pressed.

"Then we'll see. Dinner first. I don't want you thinking I'm *that* type of girl."

"I'd give my right nut for that type of girl."

"Watch it, buddy. I know how to handle a scalpel."

He held up his hands in surrender. "Okay, okay. Dinner first. I just thought you might want to build up an appetite before..."

I let him win the argument. For the record, rabid mongeese can count to four. Five, if you count a reprise just before dawn.

The next night, he took me to the movies. The film he chose was a black-and-white documentary, in German, with subtitles, and it covered the history of agriculture in the Alsace-Lorraine region.

We sat in the back row and necked like teenagers. It helped that the leather-covered reclining seats were bigger than the bed in my attic room. As the titles ran, I finally thought to ask him why he'd chosen the movie, especially when we hadn't watched a scene. Without batting an eye, he said, "Its running time was three hours and twenty-one minutes."

I suggested that next time we try a double-feature.

On Sunday, he finally let me visit his apartment. It was in an old brownstone, a few blocks too far east to be in a trendy neighborhood.

He'd told me to wear casual clothes; he'd even suggested I stick with hospital scrubs. I stumbled over the reason the moment I stepped inside his front door. Four cans of paint were stacked in the foyer, along with rollers, drop cloths, and a six-pack of blue painters' tape.

"I figure it's worth it to paint over the windows, even if the landlord doesn't give me back my deposit," he said. "I'm tired of sneaking out of your room like a college kid doing the walk of shame, and the vampire ward's getting a little old. Your staff'll be happy to see me gone, too. One less bed to make up every evening."

His words struck me like a blow, even though they were perfectly logical. "I—" I stopped to clear my throat. "I just thought you'd stay around a while longer."

He picked up a small paper bag that had slipped between the paint cans. "I tested this. It works, front and back."

When I held out my hand, he tipped a brass key onto my palm.

"Make yourself at home," he said. "Don't bother knocking if you come during the day. I hear the guy who lives here sleeps like the dead."

I wasn't sure why I was crying as I threw my arms around his neck.

It turned out, I was better at placing the painter's tape than he was. He was faster at covering the glass. Together, we secured the place in a few hours.

I called first dibs on the shower. He suggested we conserve water, and he made a pretty convincing argument, even if he smeared fresh paint along my collarbone when he did it.

While he was retrieving an extra towel from the linen closet in the hallway, I glanced at his nightstand. There was a lamp, of course, and an alarm clock with glowing red numbers. A stack of papers threatened to fall to the floor.

Even across the room, I could make out the Eastern Empire flag surrounded by a spray of golden stars. The logo was completely out of place, like a Russian word stamped across a headline in *The Washington Post*. We imperials were trained to keep all Empire documents under lock and key, safely hidden from curious mundane eyes.

Compelled, I crossed the room and reached for the navy blue folder.

"Here you go," Nick said. I jumped like a scalded cat, barely biting off a shriek of surprise. "I'm sorry," he said. "I didn't mean to startle you."

"Y— You didn't. I was just looking at those."

Nick barely glanced at the stack of papers. "I shouldn't leave them out, should I?"

"What are they?"

He laughed. "Welcome the Night? Ring a bell?"

Of course I recognized the name of the program I'd championed at the hospital. But I knew I'd never placed my documents in an Eastern Empire binder.

"That folder," I said, reaching past him.

"Oh," he said, looking uncomfortable. "I don't want to get anyone in trouble."

"No one's going to be in trouble," I said.

"I asked one of the nurses for something so I could keep all my papers together."

"Who?" None of my staff should be handing out blue folders with the Empire logo.

"I'd rather not say." Nick's tone was stiff.

"You don't get to make that decision."

He stared me down for a full minute. Then he said, "Is this really what our first fight is going to be about?"

My fists were curled, my shoulders stiff. I was biting my lip, determined not to back down.

But it was stupid to get worked up over a single embossed folder. In this city of embassies and foreign nationals, no mundane would pay an unfamiliar flag a second glance.

Still... "Can you put it some place safe?" I asked.

Without hesitation, he crossed the room and shoved the offending folder into the drawer of his nightstand. "Okay?" he asked.

I laughed unsteadily. "Fine."

He frowned and ran his hand through his hair. "I'm sorry," he said after a long pause. "Just when I think I'm getting a handle on all this, I screw up something major."

"It's not major," I protested, even though it sort of was. I didn't want him to feel bad.

"I should have thought things through," he said.

"It's okay," I said. He still looked chagrined. "Really. We should make the rules clearer. I'll make sure something gets added to the handouts. And I'll talk to my staff, remind *them* about the rules." Then, because the worried look on his face was breaking my heart, I tossed my hair over my shoulder and said, "When are we taking care of that water-saving exercise?"

"Exercise?" he asked, his lips finally curling into a smile. "That's an excellent idea."

We used up all the hot water and had to huddle under the covers on his bed to warm up.

I spent the better part of Monday dealing with disasters at the hospital.

With all those elective procedures canceled after the shuck's appearance, we had a surplus of empty beds. That translated to too much food in the kitchen and too many linens from our laundry service. It took over an hour to trim all the necessary orders, submitting paperwork through countless online portals.

At least it was a good time to review the stocking of basic supplies, with so few patients occupying rooms. Alas, in my efforts to be fiscally responsible, I'd already sent extra staff home. My familiar, though, wasn't doing a damn thing, because I hadn't worked a spell for months.

"Musker," I said, poking my head into the bathroom. "I need your help."

His yawning mouth gaped like the Grand Canyon, but he picked up the checklist I dropped on his chest. "Every room?" he asked.

"All of them."

"By when?"

"Tomorrow," I said.

His eyes rolled. "That's not going to happen."

"We need time to fix any problems before Midsummer Eve."

He shuffled out of the bathroom. If he didn't pick up his pace, he wouldn't make it to the third floor by Samhain. I resolved to read him the riot act later, when I had a longer fuse.

My afternoon was filled with a new financial disaster. Most of our suppliers had heard about the Vitriol theft, the banshee, and the hellhound. They were getting antsy about being paid. In a series of phone calls, I repeatedly pointed out that Empire General hadn't bounced a check in the eleven months I'd been at the helm, and I resented being treated like a derelict.

In the end, I won every case, but I had a pounding headache no painkiller could touch.

"I wondered if I'd find your here."

I looked up to see Nick standing in the doorway of my office. He wore black leather pants and a matching jacket, and he carried a sleek motorcycle helmet.

"I thought we could head out to Skyline Drive," he said. "Look up at the sky and see if we could catch a falling star."

I smiled wearily. "Can I get a raincheck?"

The concern on his face was immediate. "Of course. Is everything okay?"

"Any chance you know a headache banishing spell?"

He shook his head. "Nope. But I've been told I give a pretty good backrub."

I knew *exactly* where that would lead. Too tired to dissemble, I said. "Not tonight."

"Hey!" He sounded hurt. "I wasn't speaking in code. I promise —one backrub, nothing more. Unless you'd like some hot buttered toast and a cup of tea."

"With you, everything sounds like a double entendre."

"Scout's honor," he said.

I didn't have anything to lose.

The toast was perfect, hot and crunchy and dripping with butter. Chamomile tea smelled like spring. He led me upstairs, and his fingers found the perfect spot to release all the tension in my shoulders.

He kissed my forehead before he left my room. I almost thought about calling him back, but I fell asleep before I could say the words.

I got my raincheck on Tuesday.

I'd never ridden a motorcycle before. I'd always thought people who rode those two-wheeled death-traps were insane, or at least majorly suicidal.

But with my arms clamped around Nick's waist and the bike thrumming beneath my thighs, with the wind blowing my hair into the sweet summer night, I realized how much I'd been missing.

Nick parked the bike at a scenic overlook. We lay in the grass and stared up at the sky, and he pointed out constellations I'd only read about in books. When the dew rose on the grass, he pulled me on top of him, and we stared at the velvet sky until we saw a red-gold streak, long and low against the horizon.

I shouted with glee, but Nick twined his fingers with mine. "Quick," he said. "Make a wish."

I did. I wished that everything could continue, exactly the way it was.

Wednesday night, he told me about his father.

That wasn't the plan. The plan was to go for a walk around the night monuments, starting at the Lincoln Memorial, then heading over to the Jefferson and the Washington Monument.

But the night started out muggy—the first hint of DC's famous summer humidity— and an unexpected thunderstorm rolled through around nine, sending us scurrying inside the massive Greek temple that honored our sixteenth president. Dwarfed beneath the massive statue of Lincoln, Nick shook his head. "My father came here every time he visited DC."

"You didn't grow up here?" I asked.

"Nope. I'm South Carolina born and bred, from a little town halfway between Greenville and Spartanburg."

"You don't sound like you're from South Carolina."

"I worked hard to drop the accent."

"So you don't miss it?"

"Not one damn second." He answered so quickly he almost swallowed his words.

"Why not?"

"Plummer has one traffic light, and half the time it's blinking." He sounded grim. "My father was the town cop. He spent most of his time writing traffic tickets for city folks who didn't believe the speed limit really dropped to 25 in front of the feed store. On Saturday nights, he made sure the drunks got home safe."

"That doesn't sound like a bad life."

"It was a boring one. Too boring for my mother." His already dry voice downshifted into something harder than the marble columns around us. "She left town with a traveling preacher when I was five. Sent cards on Christmas and my birthday till I turned fifteen, but she never set foot in Plummer again."

I hadn't seen Nick in this mood before. He wouldn't meet my eyes. He was staring down his past instead, working through pain that had taken hold decades ago.

"So where does Mr. Lincoln fit in?" I finally asked.

He glanced up at the mammoth statue. "My father loved him, read every book about him he could find. The day I graduated high school, we drove all the way up from Plummer. We got here after dark, hungry and thirsty and needing to piss. But Dad just marched me up those steps. We stood right here, and he said, 'Son, there wasn't anyone to take a bullet for him in that goddamn theater. But if Lincoln had run Reconstruction, little ol' Plummer might've turned into something.'"

And if Plummer had been something, Nick's mother might have stayed. He didn't say it. He didn't have to. I studied his face as I connected the dots. "So you joined the Secret Service."

"I never considered anything else."

We stared at the statue a while longer. The rain stopped. A couple of tourists climbed the steps and joined us, taking an incredible number of selfies to prove they'd been there.

"What about you?" Nick finally asked.

"Me? I never thought about joining the Secret Service."

He dug at my side with his elbow. "Come on," he said. "Tell me about your father."

I shrugged. "I never knew him. He and my mother divorced when I was a year old. She said I cried too much, and he couldn't stand to stick around."

"Ouch," Nick said.

"Now you know my mother."

"Tell me more."

I shook my head. It was my turn to be caught by a dark mood. "Not tonight. Not here."

He tangled his fingers in the hair at the nape of my neck, but he didn't press me to talk. We stayed at the Memorial until a busload of overtired high school students arrived. Then we walked back to the hospital in companionable silence, our footsteps punctuated by raindrops falling from overhead trees.

Nick asked again on Thursday. We were sitting on the couch in his living room, watching the titles play over a rerun of *Law and Order*. We'd missed the entire *order* part of the show, having diverted ourselves with a session of heavy petting. I was laughing and pushing my hair out of my face when he said. "Tell me about your mother."

Now I understood how deer felt on midnight highways, pinned down by unexpected headlights. "What about her?"

"She sounds pretty unstable."

A muscle twitched beside my eye. "She's a witch."

"You know, when most people say that, it's a figure of speech."

I sighed and dropped my head against his arm. It was easier talking to the ceiling than watching emotions cross his face. I already knew what I'd see if I told the truth: Pity. Anger. A hint of disbelief.

I decided to give him the five-cent version. "My mother was a powerful woman in the Washington Coven. She was a strong witch who had a special touch with crystals."

"Was?"

"She was forty-two when I was born. She called me her oops baby."

"Did you have any brothers or sisters?"

"Nope. Just me."

He waited patiently. I had to fill in the rest of the story. It was only fair—he'd told me about his folks.

"Sometimes, when a witch is pregnant, hormones change her abilities. My mother lost her power over crystals. She was blocked from them completely."

"And she blamed you." His voice was even.

"Not at first." I sighed. It was all so complicated, but I cut to the chase. "As long as I followed in her footsteps, my mother was perfectly proud of me. I focused on crystals at the magicarium and took a first in my class. I led rituals for the Coven before I ever graduated. Everyone told Mother how proud she must be of me. Everyone told her I was the daughter every witch dreamed of having."

"Except..."

There was always an *except*. "Except I wanted to go to college. Real college, like mundane girls."

"Don't witches go to college?" I understood the confusion in his voice. I'd felt it myself, when I was only a child.

"A lot of us do. Of all the imperials, witches are most likely to pass in mundane society. We look like everyone else. We don't have to worry about phases of the moon or, you know, staying out of the sun."

He inclined his head, acknowledging the truth behind my words.

"But every once in a while, a witch is born with so much power that she's...taken out of circulation. She goes to a magicarium, but she doesn't go to college. She certainly never *dreams* of going to medical school. Her job is to serve the coven, to help her magic sisters. She's a Helpmeet."

"And what does she get in exchange?"

"Fame?" Even now, I wasn't sure. "The knowledge that she's better than everyone else? Um, love?" All these years, and I only knew one essential truth: "I rebelled against my mother's wishes. She'd lost everything for me—her powers, my father, the prestige she would have had from presenting the coven with a Helpmeet."

I thought I'd accepted the fact that my mother had never loved me. I thought I'd learned to live with the notion that I'd failed her, failed the coven, failed everyone who mattered. But my voice caught on my last words, on the crux of my story: "And she hasn't forgiven me yet."

I didn't mean to cry. I didn't want Nick to see me this way. I wanted to be breezy and sexy and fun.

But he leaned down and wiped the tears from my cheeks with his thumbs. He kissed my eyelids, tender and kind. He pulled me close, and when I couldn't stop crying, he picked me up in his vampire arms and carried me up the stairs as if I weighed no more than a doll.

He lay me on his bed. His fingers were gentle as they worked my shirt's buttons. He slid down the zipper on my jeans, tooth by jagged tooth. And slowly, carefully, he made love to me, whispering the entire time, drowning out the lies that circled in my head. I fell asleep believing the new truth that he alone could speak.

15

There were vampires like Nick—friendly, approachable, and always ready for a roll in the hay. And then there were vampires like James Morton. I wondered if the Chief of Security for the Night Court of the Eastern Empire had ever cracked a smile.

He sat behind his desk, an impeccable cotton shirt setting off his perfectly tailored black suit. His hair looked as if he'd spent a few hundred bucks getting it cut some time within the past hour. His eyes were deep blue, and his gaze was sharp enough that I wondered if he was reading my mind.

That was ridiculous, though. Vampires weren't mind-readers. They were ordinary imperials, just like I was. Just like Becs was. Nevertheless, I was eternally grateful that my warder had taken the lead in this meeting.

"I'm not quite sure what you're asking me, Ms. Sartain." Morton gave the impression he was looking at his watch, even though he didn't move a muscle. "I don't have any secret formula for keeping order here at the courthouse."

If Becs was intimidated, I couldn't tell from her tone. "We thought you could give us some guidance because you're dealing with a lot of the same issues we are. You've got imperials of all races coming in and out of this building on a regular basis. There hasn't been a major security breach in years."

Morton didn't bat an eyelash at the compliment. Seriously—he didn't blink at all. I knew vampires didn't have beating hearts or breathing lungs, but did they honestly skip the blinking stuff too? I'd never come across that tidbit at Georgetown Medical School.

I'd have to test the idea with Nick—see which one of us could win a staring contest. I was pretty sure I'd come out the winner. He was easy to distract.

Just the thought made me want to smile. The past week had taught me a lot about Nick, and a lot about myself as well. One of the most important lessons was that I'd rather be anywhere with him—on his motorcycle, on a mountaintop, in my cramped attic bedroom—then sitting here in this finely appointed office.

For the hundredth time, I wished I hadn't let Becs convince me to keep this meeting secret. It seemed like I'd agreed to that restriction a lifetime ago. I wasn't the same woman I'd been when I'd questioned Nick's motivations the afternoon of the shuck's invasion.

Morton leaned back in his chair, apparently resigned to helping us. "You've got the basics, I assume? Cameras on every entrance and exit? Electronic passcards for staff? Security checkpoints within the building, barring access to high-risk targets?"

"Of course," Becs said.

And *that* was why I would never play poker with my warder. I knew for a fact that every camera we had was a dummy; we didn't have the funding for Morton's type of set-up. Electronic keys were at the top of my wishlist for the new year. And we'd never even designated which targets were high risk, aside from our ineffective Vitriol drug safe.

Morton steepled his fingers in front of his chest. "The term 'security theater' is disparaging. But there *is* a certain visual component to what we do. You've hired the most physically impressive staff you can find?"

"Our senior guard is a gargoyle." Well, Jerome *was* physically impressive. It was only his fading memory that was problematic.

Morton nodded, eyes narrowing in something that might have been approval. "And your second-in-command?"

Becs made her voice casual. "A centaur."

That caught Morton by surprise. "A stallion?"

For the first time, Becs hesitated.

"Not a foal?" Morton asked with disbelief.

Becs cleared her throat. "A filly."

Morton's displeasure tightened the lines around his lips. "That's a substantial point of vulnerability, relying on a prey species for such a sensitive position. Here at the court, our bailiff is a griffin. When we need extra security, I vastly prefer vampires, but I'll settle on griffins or gargoyles."

"We'll take that under advisement," Becs said.

Great. I'd have to find some alternative job for Mikaela. And hire at least one vampire to take her place. Well, that's why we were consulting with the master.

Morton rose and ushered us toward his office door. Apparently as an afterthought, he asked, "Have you had any luck finding the banshee who stole your Vitriol?"

Great. Morton hadn't even read whatever briefing materials Becs had provided. Irritated by his superior tone, I couldn't bite back my retort. "Banshees aren't exactly known for their black market drug connections, Mr. Morton."

He barely spared me a glance. "No, but the people who hire them certainly might be."

"No one said anything about hiring banshees. They're naturally attracted to our setting. Unfortunately, patients sometimes die in a hospital."

Morton pinned me with that laser gaze. "I was under the impression that no one *saw* the banshee on your premises."

Becs took the hit. "That's right."

"Did she keen? Did anyone hear her the night she lost her comb?"

Becs somehow met Morton's steely gaze. My reflex was to scrape and cower like a schoolgirl witch who'd failed to master the Rota yet again. But my warder answered evenly, "I don't believe so."

He nodded once. "And yet, a banshee's wail is the loudest sound any imperial can make."

For the first time since we'd entered the courthouse, Becs seemed off-balance. "If the banshee didn't wail..."

Morton completed her sentence, clearly back to managing his timetable and getting us out of his office. "Then she was at the hospital for some other reason. As banshees are the only imperial I know that can pass through solid objects, I would assume she was there to steal your Vitriol."

The banshee hadn't been announcing an imminent death. She hadn't represented a threat to my patients' lives. Instead, she'd been an imperial *cat burglar*. I didn't know whether to be relieved or outraged.

Becs recovered first. "But why—"

Morton interrupted. "You don't need advice on building security, Ms. Sartain. You need a good investigator to track down who's bringing your Vitriol to market. I'd start with all imperials embarking on large-scale transactions that need massive financial underpinning. Money laundering 101."

As Becs chewed on that, I pushed for a little more practical guidance. "Where would you suggest we find an investigator with those skills?"

"Aside from the most obvious option of Nicholas Raines?"

I gurgled something that wasn't a reply.

Morton continued: "After all, his ability as an investigator is the precise reason he was turned."

"T— Turned?"

Now impatience swamped Morton's tone. "Raines came sniffing around my courthouse once too often. After the sixth time we dosed him with Lethe, I had no choice but to order his execution. The security guard who failed at that task has been reassigned."

I managed some sound of disbelief. Nick had been targeted for *execution* by the Eastern Empire?

Before I could demand more details, Morton offered ice-cold facts. "Nicholas Raines was investigating the Empire as a threat against the president of the United States. For all I know, the entire Secret Service is after us now."

16

It took me three tries to turn the brass key in the lock because my hands were shaking so hard. Becs had tried to convince me to go back to my office, to sit down and talk things through, to draw up a plan to learn more about Nick's past.

I'd decided on a more direct approach.

When I finally got the lock open, I straight-armed my way into the foyer., letting the door crash against the wall. I was halfway across the marble tiles when Nick swung around the doorway that led to the living room—knees flexed, arms locked, hands folded around a pistol that was pointed straight at my heart.

"Jesus, Ashley!" Nick exclaimed, and if he'd been capable of gasping, I'm pretty sure he would have. His index finger jumped off the trigger, and he pointed the muzzle toward the floor.

I brushed past him, heading directly for the stairs.

My palm slammed against the light switch in his bedroom. The sheets were tangled; it looked as if he hadn't made his bed since the last time we'd tumbled there. My stomach twisted as it always did when I thought of Nick's weight on top of me, but this time I swallowed nausea instead of the hot coil of excitement.

I stalked over to the nightstand and ripped the drawer out of its slot. Pens. A crossword puzzle. A strip of condoms.

No blue folder. No Empire flag, surrounded by a spray of golden stars.

I whirled back to the door, where Nick loomed like a bad dream. "Where'd you hide it?"

"Hide what? What the hell is going on here, Ashley?"

"Where's the folder? What did you do? Steal it from the Night Court?"

"I don't know—"

"Don't lie to me!" There. Maybe a banshee *wasn't* the loudest imperial in the world.

Nick pitched his voice low, the same croon he'd offered when he'd held me the night before, when he'd comforted me about my hopeless past with my mother. "Ashley, I don't know who's been telling you stories. But whatever you're thinking, it isn't true. Come downstairs and let's talk about this. I'll answer whatever questions you have, and you'll see this is all a huge mistake."

"Were you or were you not investigating the Eastern Empire in your job as a Secret Service agent?"

He started to lie. I saw that in the set of his lips, in the minute narrowing of his eyes. Sometime in the past week, I'd learned to read Nick Raines.

So I also saw the moment he decided to tell the truth. "Yes," he said.

"And were you still building your case when you were hospitalized at Empire General?"

He met my gaze directly. "Yes."

"Did you hand over the information I gave you?" The Welcome the Night packet. Everything I'd told him the night I dragged Musker into my office, explaining about familiars and warders and witches. Everything I'd said about elementals the night we kissed for the first time, when *I* kissed *him*, never realizing he was building a case to destroy everything I knew, everyone I loved.

He closed his eyes for a moment. He swallowed, hard enough for me to hear across the room. But he had the courage to look me in the eye when he answered one more time. "Yes."

I was a doctor. I knew my heart couldn't literally fracture into a million jagged pieces. But I swear to Hecate, I felt it shatter in the center of my chest. "Oh Nick," I whispered.

But now it was Nick's turn to sound outraged. "You went to the Night Court without me," he said.

"I had Becs." My voice sounded distant, like I was listening through a mountain of wound-packing material.

"You went back to where that animal attacked me."

"Don't make this about me."

"I would have died that night if I hadn't been trained to fight."

Instead, he'd been turned. James Morton had deemed him a serious enough threat that the Eastern Empire could only be preserved by Nick Raines's execution. But because Nick was a Secret Service agent, because he'd become the superlative lawman his father had demanded, Nick had survived. Transformed, but survived.

"You have to see that, Ashley," Nick said. "You have to understand what those freaks meant to do."

"I'm one of those freaks!" I shouted.

"Ashley—"

He reached for me, both hands extended, desperate. I looked down at my own hands, realizing I still held his key. I threw it at him, full force, and he stepped back in surprise.

I pushed past him, through the door, down the stairs, out to the street. I careered down the sidewalk, gasping for breath, desperate to put distance between us. But by the time I got to the corner, I realized Nick wasn't coming after me.

I stood in the darkness and sobbed.

Alone.

17

It turns out, when you wear hospital scrubs every day, you don't feel very different staying in your pajamas. Unless, of course, you don't get out of bed. And you don't bother washing your hair. And you spend all your time crying over stupid *Law and Order* reruns, with only a party-size bag of Tostitos for company.

Nick Raines had used to me harvest information about the Eastern Empire, information that he'd handed over to the Secret Service. I'd betrayed every imperial I'd ever known, all because I couldn't keep my hands off the guy who'd been my patient.

There was no way for me to make it right.

I called in sick to work.

That was sort of a joke, of course. There wasn't anyone to take my call. The doctors all had their own marching orders; they didn't really need me to keep things going on a day-to-day basis. Imperials arrived. They were treated. They left.

The machine that was Empire General could lumber on for a couple of weeks without my direct input. And a couple of weeks were all it needed. After Midsummer Eve, the accreditation board would shutter the place.

I had to believe most of my staff would land on their feet. They'd go back to providing healthcare the way they had before Empire General opened. They'd work for Hecate's Court or the Gorgon Council, for the Dryad Council of Roots or the Circle of Elementals.

And if patients needed to wait a little (a lot) longer for medical assistance, most of them had never known any difference. So what if a few misdiagnoses came up because wolf shifters didn't know how cat shifters treated moon fever? Who cared if dryads came down with the same wasting disease naiads had successfully eradicated eighteen months earlier?

I didn't care.

I wasn't ever going to work again.

Okay, that was my pity party speaking. I'd get *some* job after Empire General shut down. I had to, if I was going to stay current on my student loans. I'd end up in an emergency room at a mundane hospital, putting my Georgetown degree to good use treating human heart attacks and strokes and drug overdoses.

I certainly wasn't going to be allowed anywhere near an imperial patient. I'd be tossed out of the Washington Coven, too. And I couldn't blame anyone for my punishment—not when I'd exposed the entire Eastern Empire to the most elite law enforcement team in the United States.

Within a day or two—a couple of weeks at most—Nick would finish presenting his case to the Secret Service. The entire Eastern Empire would be disclosed, and every imperial in the land would be endangered.

Like a patient in hospice, I was merely waiting for everything to end.

After three days of my refusing to answer my phone, of my ignoring knocks on my bedroom door, Becs *reached* into my room.

"I'm fine," I said, not bothering to look away from dependable Lennie Briscoe.

"I can see that." Her tone was not amused.

"I just have the flu."

"Don't lie to me, Ash."

She was right. I owed her that much. I pulled my blankets up to my chin and said, "You were right. I was wrong. Nick Raines was a loser. Are you happy?"

Becs stomped across the room and turned off my TV. Standing in front of the dull black screen, she said, "Stop acting like a heartbroken teen-ager! You've got two weeks left to prepare for the hospital's inspection."

Like there was any reason to bother with that.

I kept my voice perfectly even. "For the next two weeks, I'm still a witch in the Washington Coven. I'm still *your* witch. So with the utmost respect for the bond Hecate blessed between us, get the hell out of my room."

She didn't bother crossing to the door. She merely *reached* to another place. I had to get up and turn the TV on by myself. Then I crawled back into bed, pulled my covers up to my neck, and sobbed through the entire second-act trial.

18

Two weeks was a long time to go without speaking to a single human being.

A single *live* human being, that was. I spent a lot of time talking to good old Lennie on *Law and Order*. Like a perp collared in a sting operation, I told him how I'd fallen hard for Nick. How I'd put the entire Eastern Empire at risk by telling secrets I had no right to share. How I'd lost my powers despite half a dozen idiotic attempts to bolster them—with spells, with runes, with herbcraft and more.

I confided my worry that Nick was working harder than Lennie ever had on a case. Even now, Nick could be finalizing his dossier on the Empire. He'd be reporting to his superiors. He'd be coordinating an attack by the dozens of law enforcement agencies in DC. Secret Service, FBI, US Marshals, National Guard, Capitol Police, and more—they'd all be going after imperials any day now.

Lennie only shook his head as I babbled, snapping on the figurative handcuffs and consigning me to my inevitable fate—solitary confinement until such time as the hospital was shut down around me. Then, banishment forever.

For a fortnight, I survived on food I stole from the kitchen late at night. Saltines and yogurt were my two major food groups, with red Jell-O coming close behind. If Natasha noticed, I never heard her protest.

I changed scrubs a few times. Even took a handful of showers.

Now, as the sun climbed toward noon on Sunday—with Midsummer Eve a few hours away—my TV continued to flicker across the room. I'd turned down the volume because I knew this episode by heart. My beloved Lennie was bending over a corpse in a rain-slicked alley. The victim's doctor would turn out to be the killer, hoping to become a millionaire in a complicated drug diversion scheme.

There was no way my medical credentials would ever make *me* a millionaire. But someone sure would be, after turning a pretty penny selling my stolen Vitriol.

Of course, that someone had high costs... Paying off a banshee thief couldn't be cheap. And had the same person paid for the shuck to rampage through the hospital? What was the purpose of *that* attack, anyway?

Lennie would have had the answer by the second round of commercials. I still hadn't figured things out. Maybe if I'd had a badge, forcing the bad guys to confess... Or a partner to bounce ideas off of...

At least I didn't have to follow all the rules that bound New York's boys in blue. I could ignore fancy legal concepts like entrapment. I could lure the bad guys into the open without worrying about their rights against self-incrimination, their rights to a fair trial, any of that legal mumbo-jumbo.

Whoever was trying to destroy Empire General had already proved they cared a lot about money—as illustrated by the Vitriol theft. What if I pretended to have a secret stash of another drug?

No single pharmaceutical was as valuable as Vitriol. But I could come up with something too tempting to pass up. There was moonflash, a potion that helped shifters transform to their human shape if they got trapped in their animal form. There was oakwater, too, guaranteed to arrest dry rot in any woodland spirit, and Hecate's Seal, an elixir that healed broken bonds between witches and warders. That trifecta should lure anyone with a longing for cold, hard cash.

All I had to do was pretend to have a secret stash of the drugs. I could offer them for sale at a specific time, in a carefully chosen location. I could show up with my magical armament, cast a few spells, and capture the guilty party, making up—in some small way—for all the harm I'd caused the Eastern Empire when I told our secrets to Nick.

There was only one small problem. I couldn't actually bring any so-called magical armament. If I picked up a wand, it would crumble in my hands. If I touched crystals, they'd turn to dust. I couldn't cast the most basic of spells.

But once I'd come up with the idea of trapping the bad guys, I couldn't let it go. Sure, I might not be able to defeat the lousy thieves who'd destroyed my professional life and taken away the job I loved. But if I could lure them out into the open, I could turn them over to the Night Court.

I made a bargain with myself: If the fake theft still seemed like a good idea after I brushed my teeth, took a shower, and put on real clothes, I'd do it.

Teeth brushed.

Hair washed.

Jeans and a clean T-shirt donned.

Sweet Hecate, I was actually going through with this.

The beauty of my plan was that I didn't actually need to take anything from the hospital storerooms. I only had to announce I had the goods. And fortunately for me, my Empire-wide broadcast system was sleeping in a chaise lounge in an overheated bathroom downstairs.

Taking a determined breath, I opened my bedroom door.

Well, I was already wrong about one thing. Musker wasn't

lazing around his sauna. He was sprawled in a dusty beam of sunlight, right at the end of my hallway.

"What are you doing here?" I asked, utterly nonplussed.

He skittered over, casting a sidelong glance as if he expected me to start chanting in tongues. "Keeping an eye on you?"

He turned his answer into a question. Of course he did. Becs must have told him to watch my every move. My familiar was nobody's fool—he didn't want to get caught between a witch and her warder.

"Fine," I said, because I didn't really care. "I need you to do something."

"Okay?" He flicked his tongue over his lips, still wary.

I told him my plan.

"That doesn't sound safe," he said.

"Of course it isn't safe. But I can't come up with anything better."

"Why do anything at all?"

"We can't all be as lazy as you are." My retort was sharper than I'd intended.

Musker gave me the evil eye. "Not that anyone could tell from what *you've* been doing the past two weeks. Or should I say 'not doing.'" He was my familiar, though. It wasn't long before he yielded a little ground. "If you *do* go, you shouldn't do it alone."

"Don't you *dare* tell Becs." The last thing I needed was to drag my warder into this. *My* career was ruined, but she could still team up with a perfectly good witch when all of this was over. There had to be someone in the coven who could see past the fact that Becs was a woman.

"I just think—"

"I order you not to tell her." If I'd still had my witch's powers, I would have tugged on the bond between us to secure his cooperation.

Musker edged a few steps sideways, scratching his belly as if he were brushing away mites. "Okay," he finally agreed. I hadn't meant to give him a choice. Oh well. He wasn't going to rat me out.

I reminded him: "I just need you to reach out to the other familiars. Say you saw me take the drugs and let them know where I'm going. Tell them I've finally gone crazy."

"At least the last part's true." He grumbled, but he stared off into the distance. His head bobbed a few times. He licked his lips, and his khaki shirt rose and fell with his rapid breathing.

"Okay," he finally said. "They know."

"Thank you." I pushed real gratitude into the words. "You can go downstairs now."

"I'll come with you."

He meant it. My lazy, good-for-nothing familiar was offering to join me in a hopeless battle against an unknown enemy, a fight where I had no weapon to carry and couldn't imagine any type of real victory.

"If I had my powers, I'd take you up on that in a heartbeat," I finally said.

I left before either of us followed up with something mushy.

While I'd stood in the shower, I'd tried to think of where to stage my confrontation with the thieves. I'd considered all the major monuments and the National Mall, even the steps of the Capitol. But I needed some place off the beaten path. I didn't want innocent mundanes harmed by a supernatural battle.

I'd finally hit on the perfect location. It was walking distance from the hospital. There'd be a few visitors on a Sunday, people taking quiet strolls, walking their dogs, seeking out a peaceful place for contemplation. After dark, the place would be deserted, perfect for an imperial battle.

Humming softly to myself, I headed over to Congressional Cemetery.

19

The walkways were hot in the late afternoon sun. Insects buzzed in the grass. Cenotaphs marched in long rows, silent sandstone witnesses to the senators and representatives buried in the hallowed ground.

I walked the entire perimeter of the cemetery, making sure I understood its layout. I had to know how to get out of the place if I was going to have any chance of surviving the upcoming confrontation. I wasn't counting on getting very far, though. Millions of dollars in supposedly stolen drugs was a strong incentive to keep me quiet.

I carried a backpack, loaded down with food I'd snatched from the hospital kitchen, weighty stand-ins for the costly pharmaceuticals I was leaving behind. I'd grabbed a bag of barley intended for beef vegetable soup, along with a sack of cornmeal.

As usual, I'd pulled my hair into a messy bun, anchoring the ends with a pen. But this time, I didn't choose just any pen. I used the one I gave myself when I graduated from college, the one I'd bought specifically for medical school. It contained a twelve-hour voice-activated recorder—perfect for taking notes in a challenging anatomy class. Or for making patient rounds. Or for catching thieving imperials in a near-deserted cemetery.

I would record my entire encounter with the drug thieves. And if I didn't make it out, the evidence would still exist. It would be fetched by whichever imperial was dispatched to collect my body, maintaining Magical Washington's secret existence.The Night Court's coroner would end up with proof of the thieves' identity.

When I finished my reconnaissance, I stalked to one of the Victorian monuments near the center of the cemetery. A marble angel stood on a plinth in front of a mausoleum, her robes blowing on an eternally unseen breeze. Wings extended from her shoulder blades, graceful swoops that ended in smooth lines of feathers. One arm was raised, bearing a torch, as if she were guiding lost souls to salvation.

She was as good a bulwark as any. I sank into the shade at her feet and leaned against the reassuring stone. Centering my backpack between my feet, I kept a firm grip on the straps, as if I protected something of real value. I couldn't know if any imperials were watching me from a distance.

Dog walkers came and went. The sun sidled toward the tree line. The breeze died down, turning a warm evening sultry.

I expected my enemy to appear at twilight. Magical power always resonated in transition times, in the shadows of dusk and dawn. Midsummer Eve was especially appropriate for this encounter—the days were changing from growing longer to growing shorter.

I had no witchy powers to extend, of course, but my eyes were busy, surveying the quiet field around me. My attention was drawn by a squawking crow. By a fat squirrel that chittered over territory. By the scream of a mosquito, dive-bombing my ear.

Dusk faded to night. I was wrong. Or maybe the thieves weren't coming. At least, they weren't drawing on the transitory power of the universe.

Stars appeared in the sky, the bright ones that could fight their way through the city's background lights—Vega and Arcturus and Polaris. I craned my neck to pick out the Little Dipper, extending from Polaris's bright point in the handle.

"Wishing on a shooting star?"

Nick's voice was so quiet I didn't bother to startle. "Go away," I said.

Ignoring my demand, he closed the distance between us. He wore his motorcycle gear, and the leather of his pants was fragrant in the warm evening. He hadn't wasted any time getting here after sunset. "You shouldn't be trying this alone," he said.

"No reason to drag anyone else into the mess."

"None of this is your fault."

I shrugged. "It's all my responsibility." I wasn't going to give him the satisfaction of telling him to leave again. Instead, I asked, "How'd you know I was here?"

"I've had Musker watching you the past two weeks. He took the day shift, and I took the night."

That explained why my familiar had been sunning in the hallway. Nick must have offered him an all-expenses-paid vacation to the Mojave Desert to make him leave his marble palace.

I shivered, thinking of Nick watching my bedroom door every night. I wondered why I hadn't seen him on my night-time kitchen raids. He was a vampire, though. He could be stealthier than a powerless witch.

"Stalking's against the law," I said, with more bravado than I felt.

"I've been worried about you."

"Why? Did you need a few more details about the Eastern Empire? Maybe your Secret Service buddies had a few follow-up questions?"

He winced, but he stood his ground. "You don't understand."

"It doesn't seem too complicated. You were turned. I fell for your stupid pickup lines. You passed on information I had no business sharing."

"It wasn't like that."

"How was it, then?"

He looked over my head, as if he were reading a placard at the angels' feet. "The Service investigates every credible threat against the president."

"So I've heard."

"About six months ago, someone reported their upstairs neighbor in one of those pre-war buildings on Connecticut Avenue. They said they heard a man shouting about killing the president. He set off fireworks on the roof. He wore a lot of camo."

"Let me guess. You raided his apartment."

He nodded. "The guy was a real nut-case, a total truther. His walls were covered with newspaper print-outs—Ruby Ridge, 9/11, Sandy Hook, complete with photos and string and all that crap."

"Yay. I bet you got a promotion."

"Nope. We couldn't prove he was actually breaking any laws. After a lot of interviews, we cautioned him and let him go. But we started following up on the files he'd left lying around. Most of it was the usual prepper garbage—except he was into werewolves. Said they were taking over the Rappahannock River Valley."

"The Washington Pack keeps a place on the Rappahannock," I said. I knew because I'd patched up one of their cubs after an unfortunate incident with a barbed wire fence.

Nick nodded. "The guy had a whole folder on them."

I knew what he was going to say next, so I filled in the blanks. "The folder on your nightstand."

He nodded. "I started poking around. I had the paper in that folder analyzed. It was cotton rag, really high quality. Not a lot of it's delivered to DC. But the courthouse got boxes of it, sent like clockwork, every other month."

"The Night Court..."

"The Night Court," he agreed. "So I started investigating what goes on there. It took a couple of months—they're good at covering their trail."

He didn't know the half of it. He didn't know he'd been drugged with Lethe, made to forget what he'd discovered on six separate occasions. That's what James Morton had said.

Nick went on. "The night I finally put it all together, one of the security guys came after me."

"The vampire," I said. "The one who was supposed to execute you. I know the rest of the story."

"No you don't," Nick said. "You don't know the end."

"*This* is where you tell me about your big promotion."

"This is where I tell you I've left the Service."

"What?"

He'd surprised me. I'd expected him to make excuses. To remind me that he'd promised his father. He had to save the president, had to secure the country against whatever threats he found.

"I left." He shrugged and sank to the ground beside me, dangling his hands between his knees. "Or maybe I should say they fired me."

I just stared.

"Yep," he said. "I'm the jackass who managed to get fired from a freaking federal job. But I disappeared without leave for two straight weeks. I came back insisting I'd only work night shifts. I refused to answer questions about where I'd been—"

"You didn't tell them?"

"What was I going to say? A Secret Service agent ranting about vampires and werewolves and witches would be front page news. And if there's one thing the Service hates more than a security threat, it's a scandal."

"Nick..."

I couldn't think of what to say. I knew what the Service meant to him. It was his entire reason for living—had been, since he'd left Plummer, South Carolina. He had the seal tattooed on his body. It was supposed to be his life forever.

"I've been waiting to tell you for the past two weeks. So when Musker said you'd finally left your room, I didn't waste time getting over here."

All those days I'd spent, watching *Law and Order*. All those tears I'd shed, thinking I'd been betrayed. All those Saltines and yogurt cups and cubes of red Jell-O...

And all that time, he'd been giving up the most valuable thing in his world.

"You could have called!" I said.

"Would you have given me a chance to explain?"

He had a point.

I turned to him, raising a hand to the bristles on his cheek. His flesh was cool, and his jaw was set, but my fingers felt like they'd gone home for the first time in days. "I'm sorry," I said.

He answered by leaning close and brushing his lips across mine. I caught my breath, realizing how much I'd missed him, how much I'd needed him.

Before I could kiss him back, an earthquake rumbled through the cemetery.

20

The temblor sounded like a freight train, rattling and roaring, ripping apart the earth. Without hesitation, Nick sprang in front of me, putting himself between me and whatever force approached.

I somehow remembered to swoop up my backpack, holding it close as if it contained all the treasure in the world. This was the moment I'd waited for, hoped for, the one I'd purposely brought about. But now that I was about to confront the creature who'd stolen my future, I found it hard to take a breath.

Peering around Nick's broad back, I could just make out the shuddering rows of cenotaphs. A deep tunnel had collapsed between the grave markers, a raw wound that smelled of rich, black earth.

The Gnome King stood at the head of the tunnel.

I recognized him from his iron crown and his formal robes, which looked as if they'd been woven from the gnarled roots of trees. The king came barely to Nick's waist, but he hoisted an enormous battle axe on his shoulder, a double-edged blade set on a massive oaken shaft with a point sharp enough to shift underground boulders.

Like all gnomes, the king was bald, and his face was deeply wrinkled. His eyes bulged as if he were some type of sightless grub, and he blinked repeatedly under the moonlight. His hands were calloused, and his wrists were thicker than my arms—the better to burrow through the earth that was his home.

Behind the king, a dozen gnome soldiers rose up from the trenches. Each carried a pickax over his shoulder. They rolled forward like a robot army, silent and determined. When they were six feet away from Nick, the king called out, "Company, halt!" The army stopped with flawless precision.

"Witch McDonnell," the king proclaimed. "Step forward that we may parley."

Before I could respond, Nick squared his shoulders. "I speak for Ashley McDonnell."

I pressed between his shoulder blades. I was the one who'd provoked this confrontation. I didn't need a man to save me from myself.

But Nick didn't have a chance to back down. The king spoke with all the pride of a primary earth elemental. "The Gnome King speaks to no mere message boy."

Before Nick could press his point and be cut down by a dozen pickaxes, I stepped out from behind his shadow. "Speak to me, then, Gnome."

The king swiveled his enormous head, his attention immediately pinned to the backpack I gripped. "You've brought the medicaments you promised."

I clutched the bag closer, as if I truly valued its contents. "I have."

The king's eyes gleamed in the starlight. "Show us."

"What do you offer in trade?"

The soldiers grunted at my defiant words, soft hoots that echoed with derision. Clearly, no one challenged the Gnome King without consequence. I tried not to panic as they shifted their weight, as moonlight gleamed off the filed iron points of their weapons.

But the Gnome King chose to laugh, the sound rumbling from his broad chest like an avalanche. "A fighting spirit! I like that in an enemy." He snapped his fingers, issuing a wordless command.

Nick stiffened beside me as the foot-soldiers moved. I thought he was going to fight them all at once, even though he carried no visible weapon. I cast a quick glance over my shoulder, a pleading look that I hoped he would understand. I needed him to wait. I needed him to live.

In any case, the soldiers didn't advance. Instead, the nearest man reached inside his ragged tunic and produced a leather sack. Without expression, he tossed it to the ground, where it landed with a dull metallic clank.

Nick cocked his head, and I nodded once. With all the grace of a feral panther, he swept up the offering. His clever fingers stripped open the laces, and he poured the contents into one palm.

The coins were pale in the moonlight and perfectly round. Their edges were crimped, but no image appeared on either side. I hadn't checked the Empire's commodities tables lately, but Nick had to be holding thousands of dollars of moon-minted gold.

"A fair trade?" the Gnome King asked, gloating over my surprise.

"N— Not quite." I forced myself to stand taller, to speak as if I were the Washington Coven Mother, a witch of consequence throughout the Eastern Empire. "There is something else that I require."

"You question my generosity, witchling? You dare to demand more?"

The soldiers hooted again. This time the lines did condense, the fighters moving closer.

"What I ask will cost you nothing," I asserted. I paused until the gnomes' rustling died away. "I merely wish to know why."

"Why?" The Gnome King roared the single syllable. His soldiers took another step closer.

Conscious of the recording pen stashed in my hair, I held my ground and raised my chin to demand, "Why do you want the medicines I offer?"

I caught my breath, waiting for his answer. Nick stood beside me, his body so tense I could feel his muscles vibrate. We were poised on the edge of a precipice, balanced over a bottomless chasm on the thinnest of wires.

When the Gnome King answered, his words trickled like scree sliding down a mountain face. "I'm going to sell your drugs. I'm going to send my men to the corners of the Empire. We'll offer Vitriol to children. Moonflash and oakwater, even Hecate's Seal... Wherever an imperial seeks to ease pain, we'll provide the answer. And we'll be richer than any imperial has ever dreamed."

"For this, you hired the banshee?" I asked, determined to cement the evidence I craved.

"Who else could retrieve our elixir from beyond your locks?"

It wasn't the gnomes' elixir. Empire General had purchased the potion with cold, hard cash. Rather than argue basic points of commerce, though, I dug for more details: "But why send a shuck?"

The Gnome King's laugh was bitter. "You imperial sawbones were so terrified of a little ivory comb. We figured we'd clear the decks with another hint of death."

Hellhounds were bred in underground pits. They fed on subterranean fire. Of course, the gnomes had thought to use their cursed dog.

The Gnome King fingered the edge of his battle axe. "And when..." He relished the words enough that he repeated them. "And when your patients are gone and your hospital is closed, I'll pay a pittance for the building. For the building and the land.

And then I'll buy property beside it and behind it, the entire city block. My gnomes will tunnel beneath the houses like our fathers did of old. We'll line corridors with diamond and pave our throne room with gold."

Delusions of grandeur, a clinical part of my brain clicked. *Narcissistic personality disorder. Borderline personality disorder.* A dozen diagnoses tumbled through my thoughts as I completed a hurried differential.

I considered pointing out that the Empire had debated the fate of the land for years before they opened Empire General. They'd considered a score of competing claims for the building, for the large plot of land. They'd probably even evaluated the Gnome King's grandiose scheme and found them wanting.

Before I could say anything, the king gestured with his battle axe. "Enough talking," he said. "You have our gold. Now give us the medicines and be gone."

As if we'd choreographed the exchange, Nick returned the gold coins to their pouch and passed the treasure over to me. I gave him the backpack, wishing I could warn him that its contents were useless. He hefted it once, twice, and he gave me a questioning glance, but all I could do was nod and command the transfer.

Nick took the backpack and walked toward the Gnome King. Pausing a mere arm's length away, he lowered the backpack, stopping just short of lobbing it at the elemental's head.

The king snarled and grabbed the pack. He tore it open, ignoring the zippers any civilized imperial would use. Plunging one hand in, he seized on the first package inside. When he pulled it out to study its contents by moonlight, he spluttered in rage. "Barley!" he shouted, and then he snatched at the other bag. "Corn!" He tossed both grains and the ruined backpack to the ground with a wordless cry.

I heard the soldiers shift, gripping their pickaxes beneath the moonlight. I watched the Gnome King heft his battle axe, turn it end over end until he grasped the broad head between twin sharp-honed blades. I tasted bitter terror across the back of my throat.

Time stopped as the king drew back his arm. I saw what he was doing. I knew what would happen. I understood everything but there was nothing I could do to stop it.

The Gnome King's mouth opened. Spittle flew with his roar. He shifted his weight, rolled on his feet, and snapped his arm forward to release all the terrible weight of the axe.

Nick stood before him as if mesmerized by the blades. But the blades weren't the danger. Iron would never harm him, not permanently, not with his magical ability to heal.

But the oak shaft hurtled straight toward Nick's heart, the perfect wooden stake to execute a vampire.

21

Nick was going to die. He'd given me his story. He'd offered me his love. And even though he was about to fall with a stake in his heart, I loved him back.

There was magic in that thought.

I. Loved. Nicholas Raines.

Power exploded in my mind. Energy rocketed through my body. A primal force filled me like Hecate's grace, like the spirit of the goddess that pervaded every spell I'd ever cast.

I didn't bother with the offering, with touching my head, my throat, my heart. Hecate was in me; Hecate *was* me. She knew the purity of the ancient magic I offered.

I raised my hands overhead, pointing my fingers at the Gnome King's axe. I targeted the oaken shaft that was impossibly still tumbling, still driving toward my beloved's heart.

"*Dark skies!*" I shouted, ripping my throat with the words. "*Light vies, clear eyes,*" I barely formed the syllables, frantic to reach the ones that mattered, the ones that sealed the spell. "*Fire rise!*"

The axe burst into flame.

Not just the shaft, not just the oaken stake. The blades burned too, iron melting in an eldritch fire. The entire scorching weapon crashed against Nick's chest, shattering on impact.

His leather jacket shed debris as if it were made of glass. The remnants of the battle axe dropped onto the grass beneath him, greedy flames seeking a purchase.

I swayed toward the fire, drawn by the magic I'd released. A dam had burst inside me, and I was tumbling forward, harvesting the sudden power.

I spread my arms wide and invoked the goddess who made all witchcraft possible:

"Mother Hecate, wise and strong
To yourself I do belong.
Keep me safe, all danger bar,
Destroy all threats, both near and far.
As you shelter me 'neath your veil
My love for you will never fail."

My love for Hecate. My love for Nick. Love gave me the power to turn upon the Gnome King.

I hadn't brought my tools—crystals or herbs or sacred athame with its double cutting blade. But we were standing in nature, beneath a cloudless sky.

I stretched my fingers toward the nearest cenotaph, the sandstone marker that honored the dead. Sandstone had the power of increasing concentration. It showed the seeker truth amid darkness.

My mother had taught me the power of sandstone before I'd ever set foot in the magicarium. Even when she rocked me in my cradle, she whispered of crystals and gemstones, of rocks that formed the backbone of the world. She'd based her magic in stone, the magic she'd lost for me. I could never forget the power she yearned for, the forces she'd once worked.

Now, I extended my senses into the cenotaph. I drew its innate energy into me. I let it open my eyes, granting me clear vision as I sought to fight my enemies. Looking upon the cemetery, I saw everything under a silvery light, the same eldritch glow that had consumed the Gnome King's double-edged axe.

Nick shone in the darkness, his rugged face lean and terrible as he sprang upon the king. Strength rippled off him, coursing through his shoulders, down his back, flowing over his thighs and calves and feet. He was a vampire warrior in his prime, trained to fight, granted extraordinary physical power. He threw back his head, and his fangs sparked in the moonlight.

I'd kindled my magic with the fire spell. I'd stoked it higher by invoking Hecate. I'd burst it into full flame by embracing the sandstone's power.

Each use of magic doubled my reserve. I thrust my energy toward the marble angel who'd sheltered me, drawing on the crystalline structure of her sculpted face, her body, her gown and wings. The inherent qualities of marble cascaded back to me, echoing my mother's knowledge. Marble was stolid protection and safety and security.

I gathered the marble's energy to cast a ring around our battle. Before I could say the words, though, before I could force the magic, I felt another surge of power. This one was a familiar flood, one I'd drawn on for more than a dozen years. I glanced beyond Nick and the Gnome King, past the dozen elemental warriors near the deep-gouged trench.

Rebecca Sartain stood at the far edge of the pit. Her sword glowed blue in the moonlight. Her body shimmered with warder's magic, with the force that had allowed her to *reach* to me, even though I'd ordered her from my side, even though I'd rejected her assistance.

"*Becs!*" I thought, conveying a thousand emotions in a single syllable. *I'm sorry. I missed you. I love you. I love Nick. I need... I need... I need...*

She knew what I needed. Her warder's magic merged with the milky marble band I'd gathered. She touched the border with the tip of her sword, casting a circle sacred to Hecate. She shielded mundane eyes from any glimpse of the magic I was working. She had my back, and I didn't need to waste another second thinking about the outside world.

Kneeling, I scooped up handfuls of barley and corn, the fake "drugs" I'd brought to buy some time. Perhaps Hecate had guided my hands as I raided Natasha's kitchen, because the grains were traditional offerings to the guardians of earth, long tied to the magic of those elementals.

I closed my eyes and felt the subtle, satisfying energy of the harvest. I extended my own roiling magic, feeding it to the scattered seeds. I took one breath, another, and I *pushed* my power outward.

A wall of green and gold surged into being. Corn stalks rose higher than my head, heavy with thick ears of corn. Barley waved at my knees, each plant topped with a fistful of grain.

The gnomes stumbled through the sudden crops, blinded by the unexpected tangle of stalks and leaves. Half the warriors slid into the tunnel they'd created between the graves, tumbling back to the earthen depths from which they'd sprung. They scrambled to climb out of the trench, but panic made them clumsy. A few turned tail and disappeared completely beneath the earth.

The grains' sudden growth doubled my magic again, filling my heart and lungs. I thrummed with power. I was filled with potential. I cast about for more tools, for weapons I could use.

There were oak trees beyond the edges of my marble circle. With Becs's aid, I could break the barrier and retrieve the wood, ancient symbol of strength and stability, of health and potency and all good luck.

But oak could be fashioned into stakes. I dared not trust the magic of cornered gnomes. I couldn't assume I could spare Nick's heart a second time.

Iron, then. It was trapped in the hinges of the angel's mausoleum door. I drew on the metal, on its strength and durability. Iron was drawn from the earth, but it was tamed by fire, tempered by water, cooled by air. Iron was more powerful than any one of the elements alone.

I spun its power inside my mind, drawing out a constant, steady thread. I wove the iron, over and under, forcing its shape with my magic. I thinned it and spread it and cast it into a perfect untangled net.

Throwing a desperate glance to the far side of my marble circle, I found Nick and the Gnome King scrabbling in the earth. The elemental's heels beat against the ground, a jerking tattoo as he fought for a purchase. Nick bent over the arch of his throat, drinking deeply.

I stiffened my wrists, commanding my iron web to rise above the earth. I tilted my hands and directed it toward the tunnel. I tested it with my mind, tugging, stretching, making sure it could do all that I required.

Ancient lessons that I'd mastered in the magicarium rippled beneath my work. Iron was strong. Iron was durable. But those virtues came with a cost. Iron was heavy. It was binding. It pulled even the strongest worker down.

My shoulders shook under the weight of the net I'd woven. My body trembled with the strain. I tried to cry out, but my throat was stretched, my jaw locked.

Nick! I thought, with all the power and the passion we had shared—in my bed, in his bed, on a forested mountaintop beneath the stars.

He pulled back from his prey. Turning his head, he instantly read my intention. Without hesitation, he kicked the Gnome King into the trench between the graves.

I dropped the iron net over the gash in the ground. It crushed the towering cornstalks and trampled the waving barley. It broke the marble circle, sending shards of milky light sparking across the cemetery. With the sound of a thousand prison doors slamming shut, the gaping earth folded in upon itself, closing the gash and filling the hole.

The Gnome King and his army were gone.

Becs rushed forward, but Nick reached me first. His arms closed around me as darkness filled my mind.

22

Silence. Darkness. A space filled with nothing—no arms, no body, no legs.

No. I had arms. They were lying on top of a cotton sheet. I had a body. It was cushioned on a mattress. I had legs. They ached from staying in one position too long.

I opened my eyes.

"At last."

I turned my head toward Nick's voice. "I— Wh— Where am I?"

"My place." He helped me to sit up against a pair of thick pillows. Then he sat beside me on the bed, offering a glass of water that waited on the nightstand. "I made Becs bring you here."

I sipped slowly before I asked, "How are you awake now?"

He laughed. "The sun set three hours ago."

"I slept the entire day?"

He smoothed the hair off my forehead. "Two days, Ash. It's Tuesday night."

"Tuesday..."

It was over then. I'd missed the Empire General inspection.

I'd won the battle against the Gnome King, defeated his attempt to take over my hospital for his personal gain, but I'd lost the war. Without accreditation, Empire General would close.

Nick said, "Becs brought this over some time today. It was waiting on the kitchen table when I woke."

He handed me an envelope. I recognized the logo in the upper left corner, the rough-drawn staff with the enchanted snake that had turned my life upside down just one short month before.

My heart was pounding so hard I thought I might faint. Nick settled beside me, slipping an arm around my shoulder. Of course he could hear my racing pulse. Vampire ears missed nothing.

Ashley McDonnell, MD, Medical Director of Empire General Hospital. I already knew the heading on the letter. Steeling myself, I started to read.

Inspection completed on Midsummer Eve by... I skipped over the name of three imperials who had conducted the Board's work. *In the absence of Dr. McDonnell, inspection was undertaken with the guidance and support of one witch's familiar, Musker.*

Sweet Hecate, that was even worse news than I'd imagined. "I can't read it," I said.

Nick eased the letter from my limp fingers. I concentrated on breathing as he started to read.

"The following demerits were noted in the operation of Empire General Hospital." Nick cleared his throat. "Item: Theft of multiple doses of Vitriol."

I grimaced.

"Item: Invasion by one or more banshees."

I closed my teeth on the tip of my tongue.

"Item: Invasion by one or more hellhounds, resulting in the self-discharge of a substantial number of patients and the cancellation of multiple elective procedures."

I couldn't pull enough air into my lungs. Nick's arm tightened around me, and I let myself slump against him. They had it all there, in black and white. Every weakness that had brought down Empire General. Everything I'd allowed the Gnome King to do.

"Item: Multiple complaints of substandard food for all manner of imperial diet."

As if that mattered now. I closed my eyes in hopeless exasperation.

"Item: Witch's familiar residing in ground floor bathroom, making shower and sanitary facilities completely inaccessible."

"Isn't there *anything* good in there?" I moaned, making a feeble attempt to grab the letter.

Nick shifted his weight, keeping the page out of my reach. But he obliged me by reading: "The following commendations are noted for the record. Item: Vitriol was properly maintained in an approved storage device with appropriate mechanical, biometric, and magical locks in place."

Relief left me even weaker than stress. As my shoulders slumped, Nick read on.

"Item: Medical director confirms that new staff has been hired for kitchen, notably one mundane already familiar with imperial practices who has agreed to supervise the hiring of appropriate imperial kitchen staff within the next sixty days."

"Mundane?" I asked. "What mundane—"

Nick said, "Becs said something about a bakery? Some place called Cake Walk?"

Immediately, I thought of miniature cupcakes in a pasteboard box. I couldn't imagine what magic my warder had worked, but if the woman in charge of Cake Walk was willing to supervise the Empire General kitchen...

"When did she have time to do that?"

"If I recall," Nick said dryly. "She had two weeks to fill before Midsummer Eve." Before I could babble excuses, he brandished the letter again. "Item: All patient rooms were found to be clean and well-stocked, with appropriate care for each imperial race, including solar-free spaces for vampires, moon-visible spaces for shifters, and other reasonable accommodations."

"All rooms?" I asked. "But who—"

"You're going to owe Musker a vacation," Nick said.

"Let me guess. A week in Arizona."

"I think he's planning something a little more...exotic. He said something about the pyramids, in Egypt."

He deserved it. A trip there, and to any other desert he wanted to visit. If I wasn't mistaken, I had a pouch of moon-minted gold that would finance his travels.

Nick read on: "Item: A complete security plan, including the imminent purchase of closed-circuit televisions, electronic pass-cards for all staff, and security checkpoints at the entrance to any and all high-risk sections of the hospital. Such security plan to be implemented by contract security consultant Nicholas Raines."

"What?" I sat up straight in bed.

Nick continued to read. "Therefore, taking into account all of the above—"

"Wait a second! What was that last item?"

He ignored me. "We note that Empire General meets the needs of the Eastern Empire and the various imperials residing within the borders of the Eastern Empire in a manner not otherwise met by any individual or multiple medical facilities."

"Nick—" I slipped out from under his arm.

"For all the reasons stated herein, blah, blah, blah—"

"Nick—" I shoved away the covers and grabbed for the letter.

"We do hereby attest and declare that Empire General Hospital shall be deemed an accredited imperial facility under the direction of witch Ashley McDonnell—"

"Nick!" I finally succeeded in grabbing the document from him. The motion brought me around to face him, both of us sitting on the edge of the bed.

His eyes glinted in the light from the lamp on the nightstand.

His lips were curled into the slightest of smiles. The scruff of his beard was even darker than I'd remembered.

Unable to bear the intensity of his gaze, I let myself look at the letter. The words danced around on the page, formal phrases merging one into the other. The only letters that stood out, bold and clear, were the ones that mattered most: Nicholas Raines.

"H— How did this happen?"

He shrugged. "Becs came up with the plan. She thought you'd approve a temporary contract. The paperwork is sitting on your desk, over at the hospital."

My warder had done it. She'd taken care of me. Just as my familiar had, handling the inspection while I fought gnomes in the graveyard. My witchy allies had protected me, giving me support when I hadn't even known to ask for it.

The same way my mother had been there for me. Her knowledge of crystals had saved me. She'd given me the basis for defeating my enemy in the cemetery.

I finally dared to look at Nick. "But you'll have to give up the Service."

"I told you in the graveyard. I already gave up the Service. Or they gave up me."

"And you think this can work? Your reporting to me?"

"I'm pretty good at taking orders. At least from someone I respect."

A blush kindled my cheeks. For the first time since Nick had joined me on the bed, my lady bits perked up.

"There's just one thing," Nick said, increasing the perk factor with the low rumble of his voice. "I need your opinion on a very important medical matter."

From his tone, I knew better than to worry. "Of course," I said.

He leaned close, tangling his fingers in my hair. "Here's the problem," he whispered against my ear.

My heart started to gallop again. "Mm-hmm?"

His lips traced the line of my jaw, making me lean into him. "I've fallen in love with my doctor."

"That's quite a problem," I managed to say.

He found the hollow at the base of my throat. It was a couple of long minutes before he asked, "So, what advice do you have, Doc?"

I moved my hand to the back of his neck. I tilted his head and brushed my lips against his. He was already warmed by the heat of my body. I tested his ability to follow my lead, knowing I'd need that in my Chief of Security. He passed with flying colors, kissing back hard enough that I almost forgot I owed him an answer. When I came up for air, it took me a couple of tries to get out my reply. "How about, 'Take two spells, and call me in the morning?'"

His laugh met mine, and we started the hard work of measuring out the perfect therapeutic dose.

MORE MAGICAL WASHINGTON

Ashley and Nick have found their Happily Ever After, but there are more magical adventures afoot in Washington DC. Check out these other books in the Magical Washington universe!

~

Girl's Guide to Witchcraft

Jane Madison has a problem. Or two. Or three. She's working as a librarian, trapped in a job that can't pay what she's worth. She has a desperate crush on her Imaginary Boyfriend. Her grandmother wants to reunite her with her long-absent mother. And then, she finds out she's a witch! Will magic solve Jane's problems? Or only bring her more disasters?

The Library, the Witch, and the Warder

David Montrose has a problem. Or two. Or three. Fired from protecting Washington's witches, he's stuck in a dead-end clerical job. His father says he's disgraced the family name. And instead of sympathizing, his best friend is dragging him into an all-out supernatural war. When David is summoned back to warder status, he must figure out how to juggle work, warfare, and warding—or all of magical Washington will pay the price!

Fright Court

Sarah Anderson found her dream job: Clerk of Court for the District of Columbia Night Court. But after she's attacked by a supernatural defendant, she's forced to take self-defense lessons from her boss, the enigmatic vampire James Morton. When a deceptively easy-going reporter starts to ask questions, Sarah wonders just what answers she's supposed to give. Will Sarah be able to create order in the court?

ABOUT THE AUTHOR

Mindy Klasky learned to read when her parents shoved a book in her hands and told her she could travel anywhere in the world through stories. She never forgot that advice.

Mindy's travels took her through multiple careers—from litigator to librarian to full-time writer. Mindy's travels have also taken her through various literary genres, including cozy paranormal, hot contemporary romance, and traditional fantasy. She is a *USA Today* bestselling author, and she has received the Career Achievement Award from the Washington Romance Writers.

In her spare time, Mindy knits, quilts, and tries to tame her endless to-be-read shelf. Her husband and cats do their best to fill the left-over minutes.

ABOUT LOVE SPELLS

Do you like to laugh out loud while reading your favorite paranormal romances? Then you're going to love Love Spells. Each Love Spells series is written by one of today's bestselling paranormal romance authors and comes with the promise of humor to go with your happily-ever-afters. So get ready to giggle your way through your next romance—featuring all your favorite paranormal beings. Witches, shifters, and vampires, oh my!

Made in the USA
Lexington, KY
10 August 2018